# THE POSTCARD STORIES

# THE POSTCARD STORIES

**JAMES KUCKKAN**
*Jayne Costello*

Kuckkan and Co. Printing & Publishing

# CONTENTS

ISBN: 978-0-578-86929-2

*For Mom, Dad, Elizabeth, and Mike.*

# The Postcard Stories

-Stories-

## Duds

It was one of those January afternoons where the light was fading, but hadn't yet gone, and the sky wasn't much more than a dull, warm gray, where everything was still and quiet, and a few snowflakes had begun to fall, feeling forgotten, whispers of a coming storm, where Harris sat in his new spacesuit on the front porch of his house, enjoying what would be his last beer and its accompanying cigarette. If he would miss anything after his trip, he had decided, it would be his front porch, and his chair, and getting to sit and watch the neighborhood and the fields.

His neighborhood was a fringe cul-de-sac at the edge of Mallory, Ohio, not much more than a few houses, quiet and colorful suburban shacks with chipped paint and wide, opaque front windows that lent a dioramic glimpse inside each of the lives lived beyond their pales. They were joined by a couple empty lots on either end of the cul-de-sac cluster, all of them circled around a little bubble of road that no one other than the people who lived there came down. Past the cul-de-sac on all sides were thick fields of snow; in the Spring, Summer, and early Fall, they'd go from soft, thick white plains to lush waves of corn.

There were few signals of civilization in the town just a ways beyond and ahead. St. Joe's steeple and Malone's Depot, the three-story brown and red-brick department store, the tallest building in Mallory, peeked over the skeletal trees that grew through the town, some of the last pedestrians, attendant, and lonely, and capped in snow.

Two miles southeast from Harris' home sat Pike's Station. If he leaned forward and peered around the corner of his porch, he could almost see the launchpad and its office, a structure that looked both naturally industrial and out of place in Mallory, a marooned oil rig. He'd walked almost halfway there a few days ago, as a test, and had only fallen once. It had taken him thirty minutes to get back up.

He reached into the front pocket of his suit and, after a few clumsy attempts with the suit's thick gloves, pulled out a crumpled pack of Blue Moon cigarettes and a chewed-up brown lighter. Harris flicked the striker for a good minute before getting a consistent flame, stuck a cigarette in his mouth, and brought it up. He inhaled, puffed, and put the package and the lighter back in the front pocket. He exhaled and felt himself sink into the suit and the chair.

The suit was a replica of the V22 EMU's, which had been standard issue since 2056 for all Orion astronauts and colonists. Unlike earlier iterations, the V22's were heavier, bulkier, meant for extended stays in space. The added weight and heft made the V22 a bit unwieldy for a man Harris' age, but it also meant that, if—or when—he took a fall, the added reinforcement should keep him from suffering any seriously debilitating injuries. Of course, the injuries wouldn't necessarily be a problem—getting up would. But that was a bridge, as howling and immediate as it was, that the old man had decided to cross when he finally got to it.

An alarm chirped, and a soft digital readout of the time in pale red numbers flashed 4:30 on the bottom rim of his helmet. He squinted through his thin, round spectacles, sighed and, resting a hand on the armrests of his chair and slowly standing up, made his way inside.

-

Harris stood at his kitchen table, taking inventory on his pack. It was a brown rucksack, something he'd had for almost thirty years, taken on camping trips with friends and family and the like. Most of them were gone now—either moved from Mallory, or passed. He'd loaded it with dry goods—crackers, dried fruit, boxes of macaroni and cheese—and several big jugs of water. Just in case he got time to eat.

He was about to zip up the pack when he realized he'd forgotten something. Harris went down the hall from the kitchen into his room.

It wasn't much. A bed, made, but with rumpled sheets. A window next to it that gave a quiet picture of the snowy fields beyond. A desk he barely ever used. And posters, dozens of them. Announcements of Orion Launch dates from cities across the country. Movies, fictional and documentaries, about the various exploits of Orion crews. All of them were done in a lush, simple, modern style, with brilliant oranges and blues, and deep blacks and purples, mirroring the main colors of the Orion Logo.

He stood for a moment and took a look around the room. Taking one or two of the posters might be nice... but after a moment, he decided against it.  Whoever found the house, he wanted them to find this room and its décor the way it had always been.

But they wouldn't miss what they didn't know had been there in the first place.

He crouched, with effort and phantom pains in his knees, and pulled out a box of newspapers.

The *Mallory Times* had been discontinued years ago, but as a kid, he'd saved most of the editions.  There were headlines like FIRST ORION LAUNCH FROM HONOLULU; TRAPPED ORION CREW RESCUED ON IO AFTER THREE WEEKS; ORION LAUNCHES COMMUNITY DEPOT BRAND.

Most of them were junk.  Not junk, that wasn't the right word... but he couldn't take them with.  There wouldn't be room, and they were all brittle and old, prone to accidental tear.  Harris had to chuckle—he wasn't much different.  But the point still stood.

He sifted through until he found one, a bit yellowed.  The front page was an old digital photo of an empty field that read MALLORY SELECTED FOR REGIONAL SPACEPORT.  The date in the upper right corner read October 23$^{rd}$, 2024.

He picked up the paper and held it for a moment, skimming parts of the article.

*...thirty-third Midwestern station of its kind...*

*...a great opportunity for the small community...*

*...hope to let more and more from the Breadbasket, who some say have been overlooked in past exploration efforts, join in the noble pursuit of space travel...*

*...local testing begins in March of 2025...*

He folded it with care, went back into the kitchen, and tucked it in the side of his pack.  It was the closest thing he had to a ticket.  At the very least, it could be a piece of potentially sympathetic evidence, however convincing, in the explanation of a geriatric stow-away.  And failing that, whether he got found out or not, it was okay reading material.

Something padded against his door.

Harris went over and opened it.  A plump tabby with huge glassy green eyes and big paws was staring up at him.

"She's not home yet?"

The cat meowed, and wended his way between his legs and into the kitchen.

He didn't know the cat's name, he just knew that he belonged to a woman about his age who lived across the cul-de-sac.  She let him out every day, no matter the weather, and it didn't really seem like the thing minded anyways, because he usually found a way into Harris' house no matter what. He'd come home countless times over the past few years to find the cat laying in his armchair in the living room, or pawing through one of the cupboards.  The best way to get him to sit still was feeding him.  He liked macaroni the best, that put him right to sleep.

"I don't have a lot of time," he closed the door and headed to the cupboards.  "I'm leaving soon.  So you're gonna have to find your own way out."

The cat stared at him from the scuffed linoleum floor.  It licked its lips.

"Mhmm. Right."

Harris got over to his fridge and opened the door.  He'd made some macaroni earlier in the morning and hadn't been able to finish it all.  He took out the blue plastic bowl, stripped off the plastic wrap, and set it down.  The cat looked at the food, then at him.  He meowed.

"I'm not gonna microwave it, you don't touch it until it's cold anyway."

The cat meowed again.

Harris stood for a moment, and then he sighed, and bent down, grabbed the bowl, and carried it over to the microwave, a banged-up white little box with rounded corners on the counter next to the coffee pot and sugar jars.  He turned around and looked down at the cat.  "What do you think, thirty seconds?  A minute?"

The cat didn't respond, and he keyed in thirty seconds.

He went back over to the kitchen table and took a look at his inventory one more time.  He wanted to make sure he had enough, just in case.

The microwave beeped, and he came over, took out the bowl of macaroni, and set it down where the cat was.  He stared at it for a moment before flicking his tail, wandering over to Harris' chair, hopping up, and curling into a ball.  In less than a minute he was asleep.

Harris watched him for a beat before going back to his pack.  He studied it for a while before sighing, going over to the chair, picking up the cat—who groaned with a kind of absent yawn—and sat down in the chair, reclining back.  He closed his eyes.

Harris woke up with a start.  He was reclined in his chair, with the cat curled on his lap in a warm puddle.

Someone knocked on the door.

He groaned, and carefully got up, and made his way to the door.

It was a blonde girl, with short hair and freckles, in a black coat, plaid skirt, and dark boots.  Her nose and cheeks were red from the cold.  She was holding a neatly-wrapped little package the size of a shoebox under her arm.  A ways behind her, parked in the curve of the cul-de-sac, was a long black car.  A purple flag no bigger than a handkerchief fluttered on the antenna.

"Hey, Mr. Harris," she said, a waver of surprise under her voice.  She looked him up and down.  "Going somewhere?"

"Not for a while."  He looked around her at the car.  "You drive that thing everywhere?"

"What?" she followed his eyes and turned back around, shaking her head.  "Oh. No.  But we just finished with a service, and we're about to close up for the weekend, so my Dad had me stop by to give you this."

She offered the package.  Harris took it.

"He said your Mom left it for you to have after everything. I should've gotten it to you earlier, but I kept forgetting." Her face flushed a bit.  "Sorry."

Harris waved a hand.  He turned the package over.  Shook it gently.

"How are your exams?"

The girl's shoulders sagged, slight, but heavy.  She sighed. "They suck."

He laughed, and looked up at her. "I remember mine. No fun." His fingers tapped on the box for a moment. "Where would you want to go? What do you want to do, I mean?"

"I wanna get stationed at Saturn. Maybe the C-Ring, or Cassini Station."

"Geology?"

"Xenobiology."

Harris nodded. "Cassini's good for that—that's where Brandford started his micro-terra project, you know. They've got a good reputation."

"Do you mean Hartford?" she said, scratching the back of her neck. Harris looked up. The girl's cheeks began to flush. "I read all his books."

Nothing made Harris feel more like an old man than giving advice that wasn't needed to someone who already knew what they were doing, more than he ever had. His own face flushed a bit.

He cleared his throat. "Well. Then you've got nothing to worry about. Most kids don't even bother studying for the exams now, and you're doing extra reading? You're set."

"Yeah," she said. She looked at him. His suit. Inside the house. "Are you gonna be back any time soon, Mr. Harris?"

He felt a lump. He didn't expect a lump, but it was there, and he cleared his throat again and shook his head. "I don't think so. Maybe. But I don't think so."

She hugged him suddenly. Harris put his hands up, and the small push from the girl and the weight from the suit almost made him tip over. He steadied himself on the door frame with a gloved hand.

The girl said something to him, something he couldn't

quite make out, and even if he had, he wouldn't have known what to say. So he all he did was hug her back.

"Okay," she pulled away and sniffed. "It was nice seeing you."

"You too."

She headed down the walk to the long black car, and stopped for a moment to wave. He waved back. She got in and drove down the street towards the empty town.

-

With his rucksack cinched and the shoebox-gift in his hands, he left a note on the woman's door, just a short sentence explaining where her cat was.

He wandered over to the edge of the field and stared out at Pike's Station. The rucksack was awkward, his shoulders were already sore, and his knees hurt. He put the box under his arm.

The black, scraggly outlines of barren trees and copses lined the left rim of the field, but for the most part, it was a totally flat plain, boasting nothing bigger than a few hundred humps of prairie grass that hunkered down across its expanse like sleeping golems.

At the other end of the field, a solid two miles or so away, was the thick, dark skeleton of Pike's Station. Steam vented in fat clouds from a dozen smoke stacks and shafts along its body. Bulbs of light, like Christmas lights, dotted it. Some were the green, soft pulsings of the launchpad; others were the red glares atop the highest points, markers of warning to potential air and spacecraft; more than few were the warm amber of offices and dormitories for the live-in crew, administrative and maintenance, of the station; and there were scores of white-yellows that were simply studded all across the station's body proper. Harris didn't really know what they did, but they looked nice.

He stood there for a while, cold beginning to seep into his fingertips and toes. A few flakes tickled the tip of his nose and cheeks. His breath came in puffs as he stood at the edge of the field, with snow that was up to halfway above his shins.

He took the box from under his arm and ripped open the wrapping. The paper was old, pale blue and white, decorated with little winter swirls and penguins with scarves.

Harris took off the cover and set in on the ground. Inside was a yellow note. He picked it up and read:

*Dear Harris,*

*I know you won't be around long after I go. So I wanted to give you something to keep you warm on your trip. Malone sold it to me at a discount a couple weeks ago. Try it on, spaceman!*
*I love you.*

*-Mom*

Underneath the note was a small, simple, black, knit winter cap. On the front was the Orion logo, a boxy spaceship with engines whooshing behind it against an orange, white, and blue shield, set on a background of stars. Harris picked it up and turned it over, and pulled it down on his head. A little warmth trickled into his ears.

He stuffed the note in his breast pocket, set the box down, and looked back at his house.  The cul-de-sac.  St. Joe's Steeple, the department store, sitting above the trees.

He turned back around and started, slow, into the field.

And soon he was gone.

## Locked Doors and Computer Girls

Rain pattered the leaky wooden awning above his head with the impatience and installed anxiety of drumming fingers.  He sat, soaked on the balcony, watching little rivers tumble off the edge through the slats of the old black wrought-iron railing.  Beyond and below the meager second story was a cluttered street of squat and tilting shops and tenements, cut through with neon blues and purples burning slowly in the orange of the streetlights.  It was an old neighborhood with an ambient glow of itinerant youth.

He'd been watching a young couple across the street from his place from his cold and soaking perch.  They huddled under the dingy plexiglass roof of the 44 Line Bus Stop.  He thought he could tell—he wasn't sure, but he thought, from the way they looked—they both seemed to be about his age.  Maybe a year or two younger.  Their breath hung in the damp, cool air, close to each other.

She passed through the front door and he turned around to see her.  She was wearing tapered grey joggers with bare feet and an oversized evergreen sweater.  The sleeves were ratty and torn at the cuffs.  A logo of small, white, curly lettering read MONKSTOWN STREET DEPARTMENT.

"I called the locksmith," she jittered, for just a fraction of a moment, as she said it.  Being outside the apartment, away from her unit, made it difficult for her to refresh in real time.

"Thanks.  We'll just wait until they get here, I guess."

She looked like she wanted to say something else, and he thought she would—but it could have also been just another jitter.  Whatever it was, it passed with the sound of the rain, and she sat down next to him.

She was quiet for a minute before talking again.  "I'm sorry."

Her hand laid on his thigh.  It hovered half an inch above, and even though he was freezing and numb, he could still feel the hairs on his leg raise up in response to the hollow promise of a touch.

He turned away from her and watched the couple at the bus stop.  The guy had bent down and was whispering something into her ear, the corner of his mouth up in a small smile. The girl laughed, a light sound, like tinkling glass.  She leaned into him.  He kissed the top of her head and drew her in closer.

He turned back to her.  She was drenched now too, her hair hanging in sad, wet strands.  Great verisimilitude.  One of a kind, really.

"C'mere."

He brought her in close, and she laid her head on his chest.  He closed his eyes for a moment.

"You're wearing my sweater," he said.

"It's warm."

A soft smile tinged up the corners of his cheeks, rosy and stiff from the rain.  Across the street, the bus arrived.

St. Paddy's Day, 2032

He'd gotten the call, the first one of the new Spring, early that morning, maybe 3:00, maybe 3:15. He'd laid awake in his bed afterwards, staring at the motel room's popcorn ceiling, his hands folded. He never even tried to close his eyes.

At 6:00 sharp he'd gotten up and turned on the television, an old, beat-up, boxy set that rested on the low dresser opposite the foot of his bed. The local news carried on in the background as he got ready.

"... other news, Saint Patrick's Day is today, so Leslie, what's the forecast?"

"Well Jim, it's gonna be a bit chilly today with temps in the mid-forties mostly throughout the day, so definitely bring a windbreaker when you're going out. The mistcast for today is at eighty percent, which is a twenty percent increase from the average, thanks to a holiday boost from the St. Louis Mood Committee..."

Nick brushed his teeth, shaved, showered, and dressed. His clothes were simple—an old suit the color of the dead ash at the end of a cigarette... an off-white, sad, wrinkled shirt, tugged at by a loose slate blue tie, fraying threads softening its corners... gray slacks that he hadn't ironed in months... and pretzel-bun brown creased shoes, the only pair he owned. After all that, a big blue overcoat with a wide collar that smelled like wax.  It hung, lonely and heavy, in the small closet near the bathroom door.

He put it on and didn't bother to zip it up.  He went to the bed, knelt down, and reached underneath, pulling out a black briefcase that reeked of leather and plastic.  With a small effort, he opened it and checked the contents—a couple documents several pages in size, a small orange bottle of green pills, a stiff black facemask stenciled with firm, friendly white letters that read NEWPORT THERAPEUTICS on either side, and a handgun.

Nick opened his jacket and placed the pistol in the inside pocket.  He balled the mask up in his right hand, the rigid, thin metal gills on the cheeks bony and delicate against his palms.  He closed the case.

He muted the television and sat on the edge of his bed for a moment and looked at the clock before turning back to stare at his shoes on the orange shag carpet.  It was 6:38.  The appointment wasn't for over four hours, 11:00 or so.  He felt his stare drifting into the carpet and he rubbed the dull ache in his right leg, a phantom pain from the Winter before.  His thoughts spiraled off into a kind of ether for a while, a blank space.  After a few minutes, he grabbed his case, got up, took a deep breath, and put on his mask.  His breath wheezed from the ventilators on either side.  And he went out the door.


Nick ate breakfast at a small diner a few blocks or so from the appointment.  Paper leprechauns and shamrocks were pasted on the counter and dotted the windows. Groups of party-goers lounged in booths, sipping milkshakes and sodas and talking loud. He turned around every so often on his stool to watch a trickling stream of few festival-goers pass by. Some hung out, curled forward, practically squatting, on the short curb in front of the diner; others stumbled into and out of the dive bar across and just a bit down the street. An early-morning fog had descended on the city, clinging to front porches and treetops. When he'd been walking, even through his mask, Nick could smell it—some faint cinnamon scent— and for a moment, his heart had beaten a little faster and his mind began to race, like a dog pulling on a leash, and he could feel it beginning to slip through his fingers. But he ignored the feeling and kept walking.

The waitress at the counter, an older woman with loose grey hair in a bun, brought him a coffee and took his order. After she finished, she didn't leave. She looked him up and down.

"I.D.?

He sipped his steaming coffee and sucked in through his teeth. It was hot. The tip of his tongue stung.

"I'm legal."

She folded her arms. "I'll call the police."

Nick looked at her for a moment, trying to think of something to say. But he sighed and reached into his jacket pocket. He rooted around for a while before feeling the familiar thin plastic veneer of the card. He took it out and slid it face-up across the counter.

The waitress picked it up and looked it over.

"It's not a great photo."

She didn't say anything. After a few more moments, she set the card down with a soft click. She didn't pass it back over to him. Nick had to lean a bit over the counter to get it back.

"Go and sit down at the end of the counter. Your food'll be out shortly."

Nick looked around. The diner definitely wasn't empty—several groups of people had glommed on to about two-thirds of the counter and most of the booths, talking in frantic bursts of camaraderie and laughing with each other. But, and he did a quick count, there was something like four or five empty stools between him and them. "If it's all the same to you, can I stay here?"

"Sit at the end of the counter or leave."

There was a pause, as if she wanted to say something more. Nick looked at her. "Anything else?"

"Not for you, gravedigger."

She stayed there for a moment, looking at him, and he couldn't tell if she was letting the word hang in the air, or if she just had nothing else to say. After a beat, she drifted over to another one of the customers down the counter.

Nick drained his coffee and picked himself and his case up and went to the very last stool at the end of the counter. No one even looked his way. There was a stack of newspapers—old, too, some of them almost thirty years to the date—that looked like they'd been used as coasters or ad hoc napkins or maybe, Nick guessed, some kind of wrapping for meat. Either way, he leafed through them until he found a color comics page. He opened it carefully and was greeted with a dusty puff. He sneezed into his elbow and read until his breakfast came.

He ate in quiet, looking around the restaurant. Outside the windows there were spats of muffled cheering or laughing or booing or hissing, the last two usually followed by the first two. People were having a good time today. Good—that's what the city had paid for. He was happy for them, he supposed.

He finished his breakfast with another cup of coffee, paid the check, put down a few crumpled notes as a tip, and left.

-

The fog and the crowd got thicker as he made his way down Newstead Avenue, which was clogged with bars and restaurants for several blocks. Nick made sure to keep to the sidewalk—the street had been blocked off and crowds of people were milling around and through it, hopping from one place to the next, stopping to chat with each other occasionally. Most of the bars had mist dispensers, big chunky white cube-fans that sat, humming, as innocuous and acceptable as air conditioners, on the edge of the roofs. They were in overdrive, most of them seeping fog. The whole place reeked of dark beer and cinnamon.

On top of all the neon green decorations, billboards on a few of the bars cycled through public service announcements. One of them, which took up the whole top half of some squat brick dive with *Tre's* scrawled on its side in thin red neon script, showed a few plain characters gathering around one with a black face covering.  A woman's voice came through hidden speakers.  NEWPORT THERAPEUTICS was stamped on the bottom third of the screen.

"We all know the mist helps us feel like ourselves—but for one in a hundred people, they need a little extra help.  If you think someone you know might be feeling down, contact your local Functional Department for a free consultation.  Remember: it's never too late to help someone you love."

He reached an intersection and stopped, waiting to cross, before remembering the streets had been blocked off.  In either direction, people came and went.  And just a ways down to his right towered an eight-story hologram of St. Patrick, a decoration, a public service announcement, and a crossing guard, all in one.

"Remember, on this most blessed day," the saint spread his arms wide, light filtering through his pale green translucent robes.  "To celebrate responsibly, my children.  Do it for me! You too Nick!"

Nick stopped in the intersection and looked at the hologram.  He looked around the street, the crowds.  No one seemed to have heard it.  Their faces were blank and happy under the animated grins and laughs everyone wore on festival days.  Underneath, he felt like they registered nothing.  But at least they were happy.

He looked back up at the immense St. Patrick.  Sometimes, the holograms were programmed to end statements with names, to personalize the message.  It helped people feel like they were a part of something.

He stared up at the hologram for a few more seconds before he started again.  No sense in drawing attention to himself.

The hologram boomed with a laughter that followed Nick as he walked past.

6 S Newstead was a blocky castle of dull red-orange apartment buildings, tucked about a block or so away from the crowds. A couple groups here or there were walking around, but they were mainly mid-morning stragglers, it seemed, and they all passed Nick without a look. A few modest trees lined either side of the street. The wind made a quiet rustling as it passed through their leaves and down S Newstead, tugging a bit at Nick's coat.

He opened the front door to the lobby and went to a bank of call-boxes on the left wall. A note was left on box 3B.

Please ring.

He thumbed the scuffed white button and waited. A moment later the door buzzed open and he climbed the stairwell to 3B.

Nick reached the apartment and knocked. After a few seconds and no answer, he moved to knock again.

The door opened before he could. A tired-looking mid-30s woman with sallow skin and circles under her eyes, draped in a thin beige cardigan with a white t-shirt underneath and dressed in sweatpants that rested on the tops of her bare feet, met him. Her hair was short, hanging in a careful curtain of blond strands just above her shoulders. It looked like she hadn't showered in a few days. She had a little, green, sparkling shamrock on her right cheek.  Her eyes went to his briefcase before going back to him, and she stepped aside and held the door open.

"Come in."  Her voice was low and hoarse.  Nick couldn't tell if that was a natural register, or if she'd been crying.

He nodded and stepped into the apartment as she closed the door behind him.  He stripped off his facemask and rubbed his cheeks.

It was a modest, if sparse, apartment.  The living room, which he'd walked into, wasn't much more than a big evergreen armchair, an area rug, and a lamp, all clustered near a couple windows that gave a view down into the street.  Music thumped dull from the bars a block or two away.  A couple shouts came from the street below, but the voices they belonged to dwindled quick with distance.

"Do you drink tea?"

The woman had leaned up against the opening of the only hallway off the living room to Nick's left.  Her arms were folded across her chest.  She wasn't looking at him, but out the windows.  Her eyes weren't focused on anything.

He was about to refuse, but stopped himself, and nodded instead.  "Yes, please," and then, a second or two later, "I like your shamrock."

The pause was small enough to be awkward, but she smiled a little and said, "Thank you."  She turned and walked down the hall.  He followed her.

There weren't many pictures on the walls—just a few of a couple little girls, faded a bit from age.  He stopped at one of the two on a slide, one holding the other by the waist, both giggling and missing teeth.

There was another door, slightly open, that led into her bedroom. It was plain—a bed, a wicker chair, and a little green houseplant on the windowsill. He stayed there for a minute, looking.

Nick went into the kitchen, small, but impeccably clean. He caught the sharp hint of some solution and ventured a private guess she may have cleaned it just for the visit. His shoes clicked on the checkered tile floor as he took a seat at a beat-up wooden table opposite the stove.

The woman picked a mug from her cabinet next to a pale blue corded phone and poured him one. He took it with a small thanks and sipped. It was bitter, but still warm, and he felt himself relax, his shoulders sinking a fraction.

She had grabbed her own mug and was resting up against the counter, looking off a touch past him at the wall.

"Are those your sisters?  On the wall back there?"

She nodded.

"Are you close?"

"We were," she said. She cleared her throat. "I haven't heard from them in a while though."

Nick nodded and sipped his tea. That was how it went.

She looked at him and the cloudiness of her eyes seemed to briefly evaporate. "You walk with a bit of a limp."

"Old scar."

"From what?"

He looked at her. His fingers tapped, light and forgotten, on his briefcase. She rubbed her cheek. "Oh.... I'm not like that."

"I believe you. When did the—"

"Does the mask help?"

The question was sudden, and he felt himself frown. He worked his mouth side-to-side and with deliberation, exhaled. "It's alright."

"So the mist doesn't work on you either?"

"It makes me paranoid," he said after a moment. Normally it would be uncouth, even vulgar, to disclose such information. But it didn't matter with her. "The company helps with medication, and a job, and the mask."

She smiled at him. "That must be nice."

Nick watched her before leaning forward. "Miss Curragh, if you want, I have an applica—"

"I don't want a job offer," she said. The smile almost fell on her face. But it recovered. "I'd like what I called for."

Nick sat back in the chair, slow, and nodded. His fingers traced the rim of the cup. It warmed his palms.

He cleared his throat. "I need to confirm... sorry, hold on," he bent down and opened his briefcase, pulling out a lean stack of alligator-clipped papers and turning to the first page. He brought out a pen and wet it on his tongue and spun the papers around to face her. "I need to confirm that you understand, in your own capacity, the nature of the appointment. You and any next of kin—"

"I know the rules—"

"I need to say it anyway," he looked up at her. She drew back a bit, and he felt bad. He tried to smile as comfortingly as he could before he went back to the paper. "You and any next of kin forfeit all legal recourse pending the appointment. You understand that you have agreed to this action voluntarily, and the solution will be administered by you, to maintain my employer's neutral status in the affair. Any assets and accounts will be seized in a third-party trust for a thirty-day period as collateral payment, after which whatever residuals are left will be handed over to the individual you've named as the executor of your estate. Do you understand this?"

She nodded.

"I need you to say it."

"I understand."

"Thank you, Miss Curragh," he stretched to hand her the papers. She took them and he gave her the pen. "Sign where it says on the first page and initial each one after."

After she did, he took back the papers, thanked her, and drew out an opaque orange bottle and unscrewed its white lumpy cap. He emptied two green pills into his hand and offered them to her.

"It'll only take a few minutes."

She took them without saying anything and passed him, heading for the hall. She stopped at the bedroom door.

"I don't even know your name."

"Nick."

"Nick...." She looked at the two pills in her palm and then back at him. "I'm Daphne."

He knew her name, it'd been in her report. But he nodded anyway. "It was nice to meet you, Daphne."

For a brief flash, her face brightened under the sad mask. "You too, Nick."

She went into the bedroom. The door closed, and Nick was left in the kitchen with his tea. Someone laughed outside.

After waiting about ten minutes, Nick called a cleanup crew on her kitchen landline.  He hung up and walked down the hall.

He wound up in the living room and sunk into the big armchair he'd spied earlier.

Sitting down, he hadn't noticed it before, but she had the exact same carpet he did back in the motel.  He looked out the window and watched the people milling around.  They were laughing and talking.  No worries.  Totally content.

He sighed and closed his eyes.

## The Gas Station at the End of the World

Noelle pushed back up against the main glass door, the only entrance to Big Jay's Gas and Grill. She forced it open, slowly, her arms clutching a cardboard box full of canned cranberries, frozen peas and carrots, some dinner rolls with bootprints left on them, and paper plates, cups, and napkins. She spun around and made her way to the sleek sedan parked alongside one of the Gas and Grill's two mid-century pumps, all underneath a flat, white and red rusting canopy.

It was cold, even for the early afternoon, and the sky, a light gray above, draped on the oak and maple trees and the tips of the pines all up and down Highway G.

She set the box down and pulled up on the trunk hitch. The back door opened with a methodical, soft electronic ding.

There was a faint whir from overhead. She peeked around the lip of the canopy and noticed, hard to discern through low, cold clouds, several small shapes making their way West, towards the husked, muddy cornfield just across from the Gas and Grill, on the other side of the highway. In the distance, their destination was an obvious dark shape, a blur towering on and across the horizon. She watched for a few moments. It moved, almost too slow to see at first, but after careful observation, it definitely moved, crawling and solid. A glacier come home.

Noelle laughed despite herself. She bent down again, picked up the box, and slid it into the trunk next to a few other boxes. Noelle counted. It wasn't much.

She closed the door, and went back inside the Gas and Grill.

-

She picked her way, gingerly, through aisles of overturned and torn-apart goods. Her boots crunched on cereal flakes that'd been scattered across the cream-and-brick-red checkered floor. A lingering, burning smell filled the store, like charred bacon. Probably from the counter grill for the small dining spot in the left part of the store, the one her uncles had used to take them all as kids out to for lunch whenever they got together for the holidays. A dozen or so paper turkeys in pilgrim hats, holding the words HAPPY ME DAY! in big brown bubble letters, hung from strings of yarn taped to the ceiling. Some of them had been ripped down and carpeted the floor with the rest of the debris. The rest twirled, lonely and silent, in the drafty store.

There was a voice coming from somewhere. Faint.

Noelle made her way into the backroom. It wasn't much better than the store proper. Most of the shelves had been, literally, torn apart. A forklift sat overturned on its side, a puddle of oil and gas staining the concrete in a wide, slick stain.

She followed the voice into a breakroom. The television mounted on an arm in the corner of the wall had been left on one of the national news channels. Half of its screen was dark. On the other half, the distorted face of a plain and handsome anchor sitting in front of a map of North America spoke in wavering, chipped tones.

"....expected to pass completely through ..sconsi... by six o'clock tomorrow morning. Authorities... mass... to the eastern seaboard. Analysts have yet to determine how to stop—"

She reached up and flipped off the power and stood in the quiet. The old T.V. ticked as it cooled.

Noelle went back into the main part of the back room to a pair of double doors that had been propped open.

She passed through the double doors and went outside to the back of the store, nothing more than a loading area with a rusted dock and a few dumpsters and old pallets slowly collecting mold and moisture up against the back wall.

A girl in a puffy silver jacket and brown soft boots was walking around the loading area. She'd covered her eyes with well-manicured hands and wandered, almost aimlessly, across the cracked concrete.

"Alright, where did Sammie go?" she turned her head from side to side, exaggerated, her tight blonde ponytail whipping back and forth. "Where did he go?"

There was a muffled sound near Noelle, and she crept over to the edge of the loading dock to find a little boy in a brown rain jacket crouched behind a dumpster. He saw Noelle and jumped, but she put a finger to her lips and lowered herself down next to him. He laughed with her and she shushed him, putting the finger up again.  He nodded and covered his mouth with his hands.

"Where is he?" the girl's voice was close, just to the right. "I think he's close…"

Noelle nudged the kid and slowly crept out from behind the dumpster.  The back of the girl's puffed silver jacket was to her, and she carefully came up behind, only a few inches away, and tapped the girl on the shoulder.  She shrieked and whirled around, taking her hands off her eyes.

"Sammie!  You're not supposed to—" Seeing Noelle, she blinked.  "Oh."  She put her hands on her hips.  "You ruined it."

"She gotcha!" the little kid ran out from behind the dumpster and hugged around the girl's legs.

"It's closer, Connie.  We should go."

"What's closer?"

Noelle looked at the little boy wrapped around her cousin's leg.  He stared at her, and for a moment, after meeting her eyes, his smile faltered, as if a thin, transmissible line of understanding had somehow passed between himself and her.

"Dinner.  Remember?  Everyone's waiting back at the farm," Connie dipped down, pressing her face into the kid's tawny hair.  She blew a couple raspberries into it and the interrupted smile melted into buoyant laughter.

"Can you do something super important for me," she said into his hair, "and get ready in the car?  I'll be right there."

He nodded and trundled off with all the unearned and absolutely astounding certitude every recent post-toddler seemed inexorably bestowed with.

Noelle didn't say anything until he'd rounded the corner. She felt her cheeks warm a little. "Sorry."

Connie raised a finger. Her face had the quality, like many pretty faces, of being capable of an extremely accommodating vacancy, and yet seemed specifically, surprisingly, and equally capable of searing retribution when well-deserved. It began to sharpen for a moment before easing. She waved her hand.

"We've only got today left. Just remember what he knows, and what he doesn't. If you can't do that, just try and stay quiet."

Noelle nodded. "Right." She looked around. "Did you find anything good?

Connie shrugged and headed over to the lip of one of the ramps, where a couple of brown bags squatted, bulging with meager winnings. "It was pretty bad in there, you know, but I got some frozen vegetables, an apple that rolled under one of the shelves I think we can clean off, and some bread. It's a bit moldy but we can cut around it."

It wasn't anything. Noelle hadn't any better. She doubted any of them had. But they'd just have to make the best with what they'd gotten together. "Better than nothing." She watched Connie scoop the bags up. "Need any help?"

Connie shook her head and started walking around the back. "I'll get Sam in the car." She turned. "I think Tommy and Pete are on the roof. I don't know where your brothers are."

Noelle waved a thanks and Connie disappeared around the corner.

Climbing up the rickety iron ladder that led to the roof, Noelle thought she smelled something oddly metallic and herbal as she summitted the ladder.  A faint, light song about witchcraft in Fall played in the cold and the smell.

Noelle stepped carefully across the roof, slippery from the past few days of rain and mist.  Near the middle was a heating duct, up against which she could make out a crop of frizzy blond hair.  A puff of vapor jetted out from the frizz, followed by a cough.

"This thing's almost dead."

"I've got a charger back at the farm."

"Bet."

She turned the corner and found Tommy and Pete sunk against the heater.  Their eyes were a cloudy red, and a fat red disc-shaped speaker sat on top of a box of foodstuffs between them, the old song drawing out of it in low, happy tones.

"Jesus!" Tommy, with frizzy hair, lanky in his fitted jean jacket, jumped a bit.  He coughed in surprise.  Some trickles of vapor leaked from his nose.  "I didn't think, we were—"

She waved it away and sat down next to them.  Pete, stocky, in a poofy red sweater, passed the silver pen past Tommy and back towards Noelle.  She shook her head.  "Someone's gotta drive."

"Thought Connie was doing that," Pete said, bringing the pen back and inhaling.

"I don't mind, I owe her one," Noelle rubbed her cheek. "What'd you guys get?"

"Jell-O," Tommy said.  "Some paper cups."

"Vanilla Wafers," Pete volunteered, and Tommy nodded.

"That's right. We got lucky, No—there was one box left. It musta fallen behind the shelf whenever people... you know... came through."

"Are they any good?"

"Wanna try some?" Tommy said.

Before she could refuse, Pete was already rifling through their bag. He took out the mustard-yellow packet of wafers and handed them over to Noelle. She noticed it'd already been opened. And when she slid the tray out, there was only something like ten left in the whole pack.

She looked at the other two. "You found it like this?"

"Sure," Tommy nodded. He burped.

Noelle dug out a couple wafers and popped them in her mouth. She closed her eyes, leaned back, and chewed.

"I haven't had these," she said with her mouth full, "since the second grade."

"Maybe one of humankind's greatest achievements," Tommy said.

Pete nodded sagely. "Fire, art, Mandy Moore, and Vanilla Wafers." He made the sign of the cross. "They will be missed."

Tommy laughed as Pete passed him back the pen. Noelle, her eyes still closed, could imagine these two spending eternity this way. On some foggy rooftop in the middle of the woods, listening to music, eating snacks, and making jokes. Forever.

Noelle opened her eyes. She swallowed, stood up, and dusted off her skirt. "You guys see Ed or Mickey anywhere?"

Pete jerked his head forward. "They went across the highway last time I saw."

"Alright. Can you get your stuff down into the car? I think we're gonna go."

"Sure thing No."

Noelle left the two of them on the roof listening to old songs.

-

Noelle stopped on the edge of Highway G and looked both ways. No cars had come down the road the entire time they'd been there, but it was more of a reflex than a practical decision. In any case, either way was clear. Just the gray sky and the bare outlines of trees lining parts of road.

She crossed and headed into the cornfield. It was scant and muddy—the harvest hadn't happened that year, and only the dry yellow husks, the bones of the field, remained to ever give evidence that something had grown there.

In no time at all she'd found her brothers. Ed was unmistakable in his neon orange and felt blue coat. Mickey, standing right next to him, was the second youngest in the whole group, a head shorter than anyone but Sam. He was wearing a rust-red windbreaker that was too big on him. It swelled and puffed in the cool wind on the field. Both of them were standing, looking ahead at the horizon and the shape that continued its creeping march through the fog. It was bigger, and closer, than it had been when Noelle had last looked at it. Such was how it was, she'd decided.

As she got closer, they turned. Ed had a cigarette in his mouth, halfway gone.

"Got one more?" she came up to the two of them. He shrugged and reached into his coat pockets, pulling out a bent white Madoff from the crinkly softpack he kept on him. He handed her the cigarette and his blue plastic lighter. She smoothed out the body, stuck it in her mouth, and lit it.

She took a spot right next to Mick and stood there with them for a while.

"You can see it move," Ed said. He rubbed his nose. Mickey looked up at him, then at Noelle.

"We've been watching it," the little kid said.

"I know," Noelle said back. She looked around. "You guys find anything good?"

Ed shrugged. "Some bacon bits. Half a head of lettuce. A couple onions. And a few cigars, for Don and Rick." He shook his head. "Weirdest thing. I feel like everywhere we've been, no one's taken any vegetables." He laughed and took a drag. "Swear to God. All the chips, the buns, the wafers, all that shit's gone. But the produce section... I mean... you wouldn't even know..." he stopped before he finished. Noelle looked over at him. The faint smile, left over from the laugh, cleared away, and he went back to looking at the horizon.

She stood there with them a little while longer. Her cigarette dwindled down to a stub between her fingers, and she dropped it in the mud and skooshed it with her boot.

"Alright," she took Mickey's hand. He started for a moment, taken out of his own head looking at the shape. But he relaxed, and she felt his fingers grip her own with a tight comfort. "Everyone's getting in the car."

Ed nodded and stamped out his own cigarette.

Noelle started heading across the field with Mickey.

"No."

She turned around.

Ed was staring at her, half-turned her way, half the other. He looked back at the horizon, then to her again. "We don't have to stay."

Noelle rubbed her upper lip. She looked at Mickey and bent down. "Can you tell Connie we'll be a few minutes?"

He nodded and started to walk back, wobbling a little over the unsteady ground, but keeping his footing.

She stood back up again and looked at her brother. He took a step towards her.

"There's time, Noelle."

"To go where?"

"We could go East."

"California tried to go East."

"We could go North."

"With seventeen people?"

"You're not listening!"

"We've had this conversation, Eddie, like a million times. And a million times I've told you why we're doing what we're doing. They want one last dinner. That's all they want. Okay? You don't have to be thankful for it. I'm not asking you to do that. I'm just telling you this is what we're doing."

Eddie stared at her for a moment.

"I can't believe it," he muttered. He turned around and faced the thing on the horizon.

Noelle sighed. She didn't have time for this. She started back across the field, towards the car. She'd get him when everyone else was ready.

And then she heard a sniff. She turned around and saw,

still turned away from her, his shoulders shaking.  A gentle up and down.

She went back, quiet and slow, over to him.  Next to him.  He looked at her.  His eyes were red.  He looked away and wiped his nose.

"I don't wanna go, No."

She put a hand on his shoulder and brought him in.  He put his arms around her and sobbed, choked, into her sweater.  Noelle felt a sting in her eyes too, and she buried her head in the crook of her brother's shoulder.

After a minute or so, they pulled away from each other.  They weren't looking at the horizon anymore, or back where the car was.  They were looking into the pines, the cool shade and deep green of the forest.

"This place was so lame," Eddie said, lighting a cigarette.  He offered one to Noelle.  She took it.

"Yeah," she said, lighting her own.  She looked into the woods.  "It was."  She looked at him.  A small smile and short laugh broke out from him, and she couldn't help but laugh too.

They stood like that for a while, and then started making their way back, back to the car, away from the shape, and the horizon, and the pines, and towards the old, lame, Big Jay's Gas and Grill.

## Martian Apples

Shep1 traced a grey metal finger across what would soon become its face. The SynthSkin was updated from last month's, that was for sure. Its cheeks were rosy, the thick black hair fine. All the more real.

An intercom crackled in Shep1's ear.

"Call in five."

"Thank you."

Shep1 sighed, a wheezing, electronic, mechanical motion learned through nearly three years of careful study. To a trained or observant listener, Shep1 knew the sigh would sound, still, very much like an artificial recreation of an organic, natural emotional response. But it was getting close to good. And there was a little pride, learned and practiced like the sigh, that swelled in Shep1's chest at the thought.

Shep1 stared at itself in the mirror, powdered with red dust. The dressing room, wide and white, was unoccupied except for it and its reflection in the wall-length mirror in front of it. Colonial Officials made certain it had plenty of time to get into character with as few distractions as possible.

It didn't matter. Just like every other day for the past several years, all Shep1 could think about was going home. It couldn't stomach the thought of simulation much longer. Human emotion was powerful and difficult to convey, and worst of all, there was an attachment that formed after so much proximal time with it. And it hurt, or it created a sensation that the machine could only try and classify as "hurt", because despite whatever attachment may have been felt, any perceived emotion on Shep1's account was just that—perceived. There was no reason to believe it could ever genuinely feel. And even if adequate reason could be provided, there was no way to prove that genuine feeling was anything more than a testament to its programming rather than a sign of authentic self. The "real" was an expressive capability for Shep1; it was not at all a reality.

Shep1 looked in the mirror. Wide black lenses on a long mouthless, noseless plated face stared back. Unblinking. Their apertures dilated, focusing. Its rust-red uniform, emblazoned with the blue-gold patches of the Colonial Administration, clashed with the black-grey of its carapace.

Shep1 lifted the mask from its holder and stretched out the SynthSkin face, sliding it down over its eyes. The Skin, soft and warm, suckered to its metal plating. The warmth spread as the skin did... and then it was done.

Captain Matthew Shepherd stared at the mirror. Warm green eyes, blinking; thick black hair high and tight. He touched his face.

"I am Captain Matthew Shepherd," he said, a hitch interrupting a cool baritone. He patted his chest, a thump to clear his throat. "And everything is going well on Mars."

-

The Apple Orchard in Station 1 gleamed with the artificial

sunlight of a cloudless summer day. Its dome had even been programmed to mimic an Earth sky, blue and boundless, complete with auxiliary noises such as twittering birds and, if Shepherd listened closely, a far-off babbling brook.

All this to raise just a few rows of Martian Apple Trees. They were a bit squatter than their Earth cousins, their leaves broader and a dull green. Shepherd watched from his canvas folding chair as a Farm Unit hovered over one of the trees, spritzing it with green and brown dyes. Even in this climate-controlled environment, there was still a mist of red particulate in the air, and rusty trees didn't look good on camera.

The apples were a different story—they were beautiful no matter the color. A size and a half larger than any on Earth, they flushed with swirling nebulae of deep reds and greens. Most would reach maturity within three standard months, after which a majority would be stored in the Central Freezer, preserved until successful human colonists arrived.

Shepherd glanced at the dirt his chair rested on, at the dirt from which the apple trees grew  The first batch of colonists had found success on Mars. One way or another.

"Captain Shepherd," a dull voice came from in front.

Shepherd looked up. Floating in front of him was a screen welded to the head of a Farming Unit. On that screen was a worn, bored-looking man. Bald, with pancake glasses that swelled his eyes into watery gobs. Twin gold bars gleamed on his breast—the Colonel. He looked a little irritated.

"You got the script?"

"Yes, sir." It arrived just as he responded, via wireless uplink, straight into his brain. He had the whole thing memorized before he finished telling the Colonel he'd received it.

There was a guilt in that—even the best human beings had to struggle at the simplest tasks, like memorization. He didn't. Not really. He supposed he struggled with some things. But human struggle was... well. It wasn't his. It wouldn't ever be.

The Colonel rubbed his chin. "Sorry for being late, this thing got lost again—" the Farming Unit beeped. "Yes, you did!" He looked back to Shepherd, straightening his collar. "You've been doing good work, Shepherd. Surprisingly good work."

"Thank you, sir."

"I have a letter, actually," the Colonel tapped at something off-screen, and he squinted to read it. "From a Martha Shepherd. She's sent it to us in the hopes that we'll pass it on to her son, so here we are."

He cleared his throat. "Matthew, I hope you, Melissa, Nathan, and Anne are well. It's been a while since we've heard from you personally, but I wanted you to know that your father and I think you look very handsome in the videos we've been seeing on Network One back home. Let me know if I should send you any homemade bread on the next shuttle out. I know how much you like it. Love, Mom."

The Colonel closed out the letter and sighed, an apathy practiced. His job, Shepherd knew, was two-fold—keep the actor content, and confident, for one. And two, test him. Repeatedly. Watch him, and wait for any sign of the artificial. Some kind of reaction that would signify the end of the performer's utility.

Shepherd dipped his head slightly, his eyes on a patch of ground. He nodded. "I miss her, sir."

His memories did, at least. If there was anything real in

him, it was the old Shepherd's memories, preserved in him, orienting him, possessing him at the right moments with the right words and actions. They weren't his own... but he treasured them. They gave him the opportunity to feel what it was like to feel—even if the sensation was fleeting and dispossessed.

The Colonel's grey eyes lingered on him for a moment, but he nodded. "The next supply shuttle's due to leave in a month or so. In a couple years, you'll be get a taste of Ma's homemade bread again." There was genuine sentiment in the words, but the last few ended in a kind of dry, drawn-out—minutely, but it was there, Shepherd could hear it—drawl. A cold humor that emerged any time one of the Officials had to pretend along with him.

A voice called from off-camera. The Colonel leaned forward to get a better ear of it.

"What? Okay, alright. Yes. ALRIGHT." He went back to Shepherd.

"Alright, Captain," the Colonel leaned back, typing in a few commands off-screen. "We need to keep this shoot on schedule. Ready to start?"

"Yes, sir."

Rows and rows of humble little apple trees underneath a wide blue sky.

A handsome man walked into frame, his brick-red Colonial Administration uniform as crisp as the black in his hair and the green in his eyes.

"You know," he said, walking along the rows. "If there's one thing I love about Mars, it's the possibility. This planet can be anything you want it to be—and you could be the same."

He stopped, inhaling deeply, hands on his hips, a soft smile on his face.

"Back on Earth, I was a soldier. 415th Mechanized Infantry. I saw combat in all the theaters of the Peninsular Wars. I fought for my country. I saw friends die for my country, like so many of us. And before the end, before the Colonial Treaty, before we learned to forgive each other and reach for something higher—together—I remember looking up at the stars that September night before we took Pyongyang. And I remember thinking: 'What am I going to be after all this is over? What *could* I be?'"

The man looked out, beyond the rows of apple trees.

"Well, the Colonial Administration had an answer: more. I could be more, my family could be more—all of us can be more. And now look where I am!"

He spread his arms, a huge smile on his face that broke into a laugh. "I'm a farmer on Mars, growing some of the best darn apples you'll ever eat!"

The man picked one of the fruits from the trees and raised it to his mouth—

But not before a quick young hand snatched it away. A freckled kid with tousled black hair ran away, apple in hand, laughing, taking a big bite as he did.

"Nathan!" the man chuckled, catching his son before he could go too far. "C'mere you!"

A beautiful blonde woman in a housedress came out from

behind the trees, holding the delicate hand of a little girl with chestnut hair in a blue, simple dress.  The woman crouched down to the little girl.

"Go on," she whispered with a smile.

And the girl ran, giggling, tackling her father over, who gave in with a "Whoaaa no!" and flopped on the ground.

They were all there in a heap, laughing, wrestling.

"Hey!" the woman called.  The three-headed heap looked up—Mom was now holding a wicker basket swollen with apples.  She hefted it and raised an eyebrow.

The little boy and girl bounced off, flying to her.  They made a grab for the fruit, but the mother held the basket a bit out of their reaches.  She gave them a stern look with a warm smile, and the two calmed down and waited, momentarily patient.

She bent down and gave them their pick.  They dove in.

"Just one, Nathan, just one!  Leave some for Anne, come on now!" the woman chuckled.  Her husband walked over and slipped a hand around her waist.  She smiled up at him.  And he smiled back at her, then looked out in front of him.

"If you want more than a taste of what you can be, think Mars," he hefted an apple, staring at it for a moment before taking a big, gulping bite, juice trickling down his cheek and off his chin.

He smiled even wider, his cheeks shiny and full with pulp.  "A planet of possibility!"

And he held that smile for a few moments, staring....

"Aaaand CUT!  Perfect."

A bell rang out, and a Farming Unit hovered over with a bucket.  Shepherd considered it for a moment, then spit out the fruit.  He still kept the apple, though, turning it over in his hand, looking at the bite mark, at the dent he'd put in the perfect red-green skin he couldn't taste.

Already, Mel2, Nat3, and Anne7 were stripping off their SynthSkin masks with the help of a few Farming Units.  Mel2 glanced over at him, staring at the apple.

"Hey," she said.  Her voice was remotely feminine, but filtered.  "You're keeping it on?"

He nodded, looking at the apple for a bit longer.  "Helps me stay in character."  He managed a smile.

She observed him for a moment, apertures dialing in and out.  "If you ever want to practice, let me know.  I could keep mine on too."

"Sure thing, Mel."

Shepherd separated himself from the group, taking a moment to nod at the Colonel's Farming Unit, which was in discussion with Nat3.  The Colonel nodded back and just like that, the last gauntlet of the day was past.  All he'd have to do was keep doing this, forever, or until the Administration got real human beings in to take his place.  Whichever was the most cost-effective at this point.

He stopped for a moment—below one of the trees, under the cool shade of the artificial sun, lay a small basket of just a few apples.  Recently picked, he assumed.

Shepherd looked around.  Everyone was absorbed in their own business.

He bent down and picked up the basket, quietly walking off the farm set.  It wasn't illegal or against the rules for the actors to take things from the set—all they had to do was ask.  But Shepherd wasn't in the mood, because asking meant a whole battery of inquiry he didn't have the time or the energy for.  He had other things on his mind.

—

Shep1 walked down one of the Western Arm of the First Colony, a long, smooth, white, vaulted corridor, a great and empty mausoleum.  It passed by a few touches that had been recreated to add a bit of humanity.  Old Roman busts, huge and crowded Renaissance paintings of markets and saints, a few neon-pastel Modern artworks—the Western Arm exhibit had been made to fit its orientation.

Near the end, there was even a projector playing a film, a whirring black and white reel that took up a good forty feet of wall.  A scene played in silence, cowboys in a stagecoach trying to outrun Indian Braves.  Shep1 had seen this one before.

It stopped and watched for a moment.

—

A harsh cough and a rattling breath.

"You're home."

Shepherd shut the door carefully, balancing the bushel of apples against his hip.  He'd hoped to let her sleep a little bit longer—but she was alert.  As ever.

"That's right," he turned, putting on a smile.

There she was, a little lump, curled under a coarse, thin blanket on his flat, tough bed.  Her fingers drew the covers up a little more, with exhausted eyes and a glint that betrayed a perception that came and went with youth.  Her blonde hair fell in tangles—he'd have to help her wash it again, soon. Maybe tomorrow morning before he left.

"You have to go back?" she said as he went over to the sink and ran cool water over the bushel. The apples gleamed in a bloody light under the water.

He laughed. "Nope. All done for today."

"Good," and even though his back was turned, he could see that firm upper lip, the commanding nod. And he couldn't help but laugh again.

"What's so funny?"

"Nothing, hon. Nothing." He shut the tap off and brought the bushel over to her, sitting on her bed.

She eyed the fruit. "Fresh?"

"Just about," he said, offering one. She scrunched her mouth up, contemplating... then took it, barely able to wrap a single hand around the apple. A small bite followed, and then another. For a few minutes, the two ate in silence.

"Mom and Nathan are still sick?"

Shepherd slowed his chewing. He looked over to her—she'd set her apple down, letting it roll between a gap in her knees under the covers.

"They're getting better," he finally said. She looked him up and down, and then she nodded.

"Alright." She started eating again, this time fully absorbed in the act.

He watched her for a beat before returning to his own apple.

"How are you feeling?"

She shrugged thin shoulders, another cough pushing from her chest. "Okay."

"Better than yesterday?"

"I think so."

Shepherd extended a hand and laid it flat on her forehead. She looked up at him. She was warm.

"Hey?"

She looked into his, her cheeks brimming with pulp. She kept chewing.

"I love you. You know that, right?"

Anne swallowed and smiled, rolling her eyes, and for a moment he saw her possible future, the makings of a mature woman stitched into the face of a little girl. "I know, Dad." Then concern weighed her brows down. "You feel cold. Are you okay?"

He gave a laugh and drew his hand back. She'd felt what was underneath the skin. "I'm alright. They keep it cold in the Dome. You aren't cold at all, are you?"

She thought for a moment, and a tiny shiver passed through her shirt. "Maybe a little."

"Well, let's see what we can do about that."

He went over to the heating unit and keyed in a few commands, raising the temperature. The machine ca-chunked into gear, and a low hum followed. Shepherd went back over to the bed, this time lying down next to Anne. "Better?"

She nodded, turning over on her side, eyes watery in the low light of the cabin. "Yeah..."

"Yeah what?"

"Well..."

"Well what?"

"Dad!" she laughed, batting him on the arm. "Can you tell a story?"

"Oh..." Shepherd rubbed his chin, sucking in through his teeth, peering through a furrowed brow. "Well, I don't know."

"Please! Please please please!"

"Alright, okay, okay, don't hurt yourself," Shepherd laughed. "You've convinced me. Now, a story, a story...."

And he told her a story, not a great one, but little girls don't need their Dads to tell great stories.

He told her about brave explorers from a far-away world who traveled to make a better place for the people they'd left back home. None of the explorers would grow up—they'd be the same age, forever, once they reached the new world, and no one knew why.

But when they got to the new world, they found a princess there. She was small, but one day, she'd be big, and she'd be Queen of the whole world. She was the reason they'd come.

So one of the explorers, her Dad, the bravest and best out of everyone, ever, I mean, really, really great—Dad!—would come and visit her while all the other explorers were working. He'd bring her apples and stories, and he'd stay with her to make sure she'd get to grow up. And someday she would. And he couldn't wait to see her when she did.

Shepherd looked over. Her eyes were shut, and little breaths rose the blankets up and down... up and down...

He pulled them a bit more snug, and she shifted, extending a hand to his, fingers lacing themselves with his own.

He was a little cold still, like the ship she'd been on with him and Mom and Nate. She'd wander down the hallways sometimes, when her and Nate would play hide 'n seek, and she'd test spots on the walls, to see if they were warm at all. There was so much light outside from the stars, how could they be cold? But they were. Just like him.

He wasn't her Dad. She knew that. But he was here with her, and she felt sad for him, so she liked him.

"You don't feel so cold anymore..." her eyes opened a bit, and a half-smile creased her face. She sighed, and fell back asleep.

Shep1 laid there for a while, and for a moment, he too drifted off to sleep.

## Berg 43

A crowd had gathered around Bergstaðastræti 43 to watch it burn.  Warm, licking flames pooled out from the windows and the doors of the gray, tilted tenement, a skull leaking into the sky.

Sgt. Frank Baum sat on the curb, curled forward, a hulking beetle in his body armor.  He was trying to light a cigarette. The faint wind that blew down the street, cold, and briny, just off the Atlantic, kept snuffing out the flame.  And his gloves were too thick to properly flick the sparkwheel.  He tried for a full minute before it finally caught.  Baum took a drag and blew, watching the crowd.  Their faces were a vacant interest. The fire cast their shadows in long and warbling silhouettes against the apartment buildings and storefronts behind them.

Several other troopers, who'd arrived from the Precinct a few minutes ago, had already formed a loose perimeter, keeping the crowd to half the street and the other sidewalk.  The word PENS was stamped in bold white across the backs of their armor.

His eyes drifted from them to another group of troopers, who were loading a dozen or so cardboard boxes overflowing with papers and banners and electronics into a crimson armored truck.  Psychonautic Event Nullification Squad was printed, bold again, under the logo of a circle split in half, one half red, the other blue.

"Excuse me."

Baum turned to his right.  A tall, spindly, younger man in a long black coat was standing a foot or so away, hands in his pockets.  His hair was tight on the sides, but long on the top, a fine feathered blond nest.  He extended a hand and smiled.  His teeth were pleasantly crooked.

"Óskar Guðmarsdóttir.  I am the Reykjavik Precinct's Domestic Liaison."

Baum bent forward a bit and shook the guy's hand.  He'd met Domestic Liaisons at other postings before.  They were usually needling and anxious, but they did their jobs, and they rarely got in the way.  He felt almost a kind of paternal care for the guys like Oskar.  Baum patted the section of curb next to him and, after a moment's hesitation, Óskar sat down.

"Smoke?"

Óskar nodded and Baum reached into his jacket and pulled out his pack.  He handed them to Óskar, who rifled through, picked one out, and accepted Baum's lighter.  He lit and leaned back a bit on the palms of his hands.

"It is a nicer night than I thought it would be." The Icelander's English was clipped and had that lilting Scandinavian tone that conveyed a sort of foreign confidence.  Baum had to smile a bit, and he nodded.

"Cold.  But still nice," he said.  The fire roared behind them.

Óskar puffed and leaned forward, nodding towards the men carrying the boxes to the truck.  They were almost finished.

"This was an S17?"

"Yes, it was."

"What did you find?"

Baum looked at him for a moment. The kid, and he did look like a kid, had the eyes of someone who had never been so close to a kind of blooming terror. There was a naïve excitement mixed with a humble fear knit across the lines of his face and brow.

Baum sighed, sniffed, and rubbed his nose. "Óskar, have you ever heard of Charles Manson?"

The other man shook his head.

Baum whistled. "He was a piece of work. And not that this'll mean much to you, but this guy was like if Chuck was more popular, and well-armed, and patient. Real patient." He took a puff and continued, the smoke and words rolling out from behind his teeth and tongue in one.

"Ten years from now his cult woulda had a network from here to Athens, no stops, no brakes. A root system of fanatics who look just like you and me," Baum bounced a big gloved pointer finger between himself and Óskar. "All of them ready, at a sign, to throw every major population center on the continent into blackout. Total panic. Heads on pikes and blood in the storm drains. A real S17. That was the scenario." He scratched his head. "And we found exactly what the PAIS Console gamed out. This guy was Black Front. He's got invoices for materiel headed to twenty-odd countries. Banners and flags, explosives, body armor, all homemade. God knows what's on his hard-drive. God knows what he was able to get off of it before we showed up." Baum inhaled and blew smoke, looking up at the stars. He still couldn't believe, in the biggest city in the country, he could still see the white-purple bands of old European stars arcing over his head. Somehow, they really did look older than the ones back home. He shook his head and took another puff. "He even made his own PAIS."

Oskar coughed. He looked at Baum. "You're sure?"

"Check the truck," Baum said. "It's in there somewhere."

"Could there be others? Copies?"

"I don't think so."

But Óskar had stood up, half a cigarette tight in a loose vice between his pointer and middle fingers. "I need to report to the Home Office. That.... In the hands of fanatics...." He rubbed his forehead, the ember and smoke of his cigarette coming dangerously close to his hair. "Can you give testimony if necessary?"

Baum nodded. "You know where to find me."

Óskar reached his hand out. Baum shook it, and the Icelander left.

Baum watched him go and couldn't help but chuckle. He went back to watching the crowd.

There was a calm warmth on his face. He felt detached, as the fire roared behind, and the curious faces of the crowd, blue and orange in the dark and the fire, looked past him.

Half an hour before, just a few minutes after the fire had been set, he'd just sat down and seen a young boy, maybe no more than fourteen, watching from the back. And there had been something, something in him, that had clicked. He'd watched the boy watch the fire. Seen a kind of change in the kid's eyes. In his jaw. And he'd kept watching as the youth, hands in pockets, walked quickly away from the scene as more onlookers came by.

And Baum had known, in that moment, they'd gotten the wrong guy.

## The Midnight God

The Beaufort Diner was one of the only places Isabelle Mendes had ever been to that still let patrons smoke inside—and for that, she'd always be grateful.  It made her feel like an old detective.  It added a pretense of purpose to her day.

She lounged back in the cushy maroon booth, legs dangling off the end, and took out a Madoff Menthol from the green pack near a plain white ashtray on the table and lit it.  She inhaled and breathed out, watching the cloud roll in the low incandescent lights of the diner.

Isabelle took a look around.  Her only company were a few old men in flannels and stained pale blue jeans at the end of the counter, and the waitress chatting with them.  Above them, an old analog clock with a rooster on the face hung on the wall.  It was four-fourteen.  Isabelle sighed and turned her head around, craning to look out the window at her back.

The diner sat on the end of the Hot Springs Main Street.  Outside, the sky was black, a few stars mingling with streaks of clouds.  A car passed outside the window, heading out into the expanse of quietly rolling plains that continued for miles beyond the edge of the town.

Her coffee cup, steaming a bit, sat on its saucer in front of her.  She'd tested, with a quick grip around the body, to see if it'd cooled down. Good enough. She took a sip. It was bitter, but warm, and she was glad to have something in her. She wasn't hungry, but she still felt the need to have something other than smoke, and the drink filled her up enough.

The door at the end of the diner opened and its bell jingled. She peeked over the top of her booth.

A tall man in a long grey coat, carrying a thin briefcase, had come in. He exchanged a few words with the guys at the counter, and headed her way. The guy had sturdy oak features, but his whole frame drooped like a weeping willow. His evergreen tie hung loose around his neck, and under his eyes were dark rings. Just wrapping the upper curve of his right cheek was a faint birthmark the size of a thumb.

"Morning Is," he sank into the opposite end of the booth. He set the briefcase next to him, propping it up.

"Mornin'," she sat up, swinging her legs over the edge and onto the floor. She leaned forward a bit. "I didn't know when you'd be here, so—"

"It's alright," he waved his hand. The waitress behind the counter, a younger woman with lines in her face and black close-cut hair, came up to the booth.

"Mornin' hon. Coffee?"

"Yes, please."

"You take anything in it?"

"Just black's fine. Thank you."

The waitress smiled and walked back behind the counter.

"So," Isabelle leaned back and crossed her legs under the table. "Where are we goin'?"

The man was rooting around in his suitcase and pulled

out a slim stack of papers clipped together.  He set them on the table and slid them over to Isabelle.

"Recognize this?"

She picked them up and flipped through.

PP-248730

SA

*PP-248730*

WO Type: PM          Location ID: 0069-9999(Entire Building – 9999)     Request #: 8888
Subtype:                  Facility:  Hot Springs, MT                          Reference #:
WO Placed On:  Asset        Building: Main Office Bldg                  Status: Created by PM Schedu
Primary Ph:                 Floor:                                      Requested: 6/17/2006
Requestor:  PM Schedule     Department:                                 Est. Start:
Requestor Ph:               Priority:  1 – Routine                      Est. End: 6/17/2006 00:00
Repair Center:  Lower Office   Completed:
Acct No: 1010319073          Project:  -                                Modified By: khimori
Asset ID: PROCESSOR   Commodore Amiga 1000 - 1985                       Time: 6/17/2006 07:30
Risk Level:                 Supervisor: Matthew Rubarch                 Total Hours:
Sub location:                                                           Mfr:
Model:                       VIN/Serial #:
Last Date Not Located:                       Not Located Count:
Action Requested: Z – PM – Anomaly Detection, 0 Factor, Annual
Comments:
Svc Interruption:

Code: Z10070 – Z PM – Anomaly Detection, 0 Factor, Annual       Task Due Date: 6/17/2006 00:00
Failure Code:
Failure Sub Code:                                              Completion date:
Authorized By:                                                Finished Date:
Contractor:
Trade: 00 – Anomaly Detection                                  WO #: PP-248730
                                                              PM Interval: 1Year

(PP-248730/Z10070 – Z PM – Anomaly Detection, 0 Factor, Annual)

Intake:

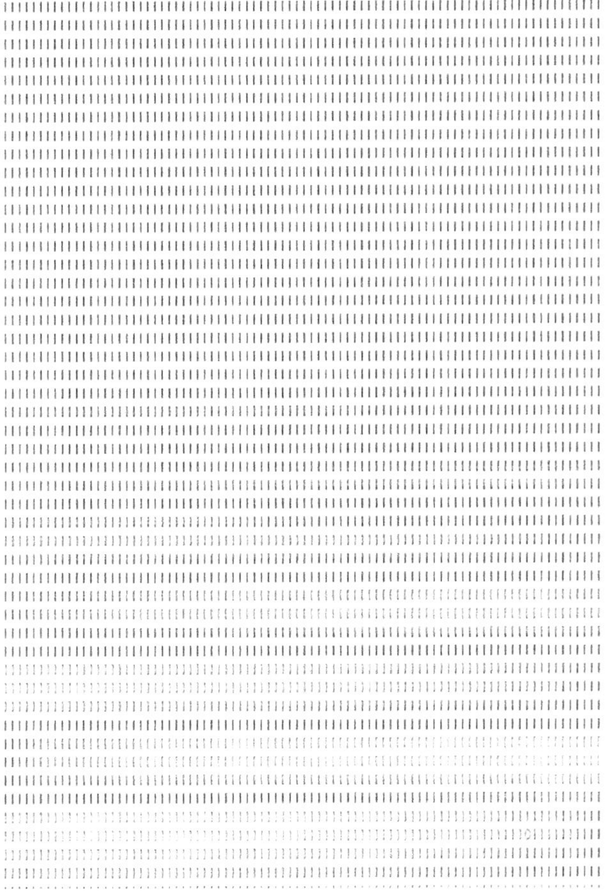

"Oh shit," her eyes caught on the zero in the bottom right third row. "I must've missed.... I'm sorry—"

The waitress came back to the booth with a dirty silver carafe, a saucer, and a little white ceramic mug. She poured the coffee in. "You two want anything to eat?"

Rubarch held his hand up. "We're alright, thank you."

"Alright. Let me know if you change your minds."

She left them again.

"Matt—"

"Is, it's fine," Rubarch drank a little of his coffee before wincing. "Wow that's hot." He set the cup back down and tucked the papers back into his briefcase. "I'm just glad I caught it." He looked at her for a moment and something in his eyes changed. "I heard you were quitting."

Isabelle blinked. She took one last puff on her cigarette and snubbed it in the ashtray. She exhaled and nodded. "Yeah."

"Found something else?"

She nodded and traced circles in the table with her index finger. "Optics VI hired me for an analyst job. It's down in Boseman. I'll be closer to home."

"Excited?"

"Sad, actually," she said, looking up at him.

"You sound surprised."

"I am," she laughed a bit. "I'm ready for something else.... But it's gonna be hard to leave."

"Ah," Rubarch shook his head. "You won't forget it."

He tested his coffee, picked it up, and drank a couple sips. He set the cup down and wiped his mouth with the back of his hand. "Mind if I—?"

"Oh, no, yeah," she tipped a cigarette out of her pack and handed it and her lighter to him.  He caught the end with a quick flame and inhaled deep, spreading his arms out on the back of the booth.

"I never asked," Isabelle lit her own and sat back a little, letting herself relax into the booth.  "How long have you been here?"

"Ten years."

"Wow."

"I know.  I'm old."

"Ever think about leaving?"

"Every day," Rubarch nodded, and he chuckled, quiet. "Every day.  But..." he shrugged.  "I don't know.  I don't mind the early mornings.  And not always being in the office, that's something."

The two of them talked for another half hour, exchanging words and smoke in the small diner, before Rubarch stood up, paid the check, and they left.

-

The rabbit's eyes were a milky white.  Isabelle squatted down and ran her finger over the disposable camera's shutter button.  She snapped a photo, wound the film, and snapped another one.  Spots shone in her eyes from the white punch of the flash, and as she got up from her squat, she rubbed her eyes, groaning.

It occurred to her, like it always had over the past year, how eerie the quiet at a site could be. It wasn't like the noise was minimal—there just wasn't anything there. No wind. No bugs flying around, no crickets or birds. Never even a car. Everything seemed to naturally avoid the sites.

She stowed the camera in her jacket pocket and, as she walked down the hill, careful to mind the wet slickness of the dew in the grass, pulled her jacket closer. The morning was cold, and she could see her breath in faint wisps from her mouth, small curling trails that disappeared almost the instant they came.

Isabelle headed down the modest slope of the hill and across the plain. A hundred feet away or so sat a '92 JEEP Cherokee, deep green with wood paneling, Rubarch's personal relic. It was at the end of a dirt road that continued through calm, gentle hills and disappeared after about a quarter mile.

Rubarch was sitting on the edge of a small stone totem, a short limestone obelisk on a rough-hewn cobblestone square. He had a set of ancient beige over-ear headphones on and was scrolling through a blocky laptop.

Isabelle sat down next to him. He looked up and pulled the headphones down. The light from the monitor played under his eyes. "Did you get the photos?"

"Mhmm."

"Just hang on to the camera for now. I'll log them when I get back to the office."

Isabelle nodded and watched him. He was buried in his monitor. His lips worked noiselessly. He looked like a little boy, and she smiled for a moment as she pulled out a cigarette, lit, and blew.

"What's up?"

Rubarch looked over and pulled the headphones down. "Hm?"

"I said, 'What's up?'"

"Something's off with the reading," he said, half to her, half to the screen. He turned back and scrolled through the readout. "We found what died. But it's still flashing. It hasn't disappeared yet."

"Maybe there's a bit of lag."

"Maybe."

Rubarch went back to the screen, slowly, absently pulling the headphones back over his ears.

Isabelle looked away from him, putting both hands out behind her, and leaned back. The morning sky was beginning to lighten with the coming sunrise. Yellow and orange tinged the fading blue on the horizon, throwing up a sea-green tint onto everything. She inhaled and blew out and decided, even if it was eerie, she was happy for the quiet.

She shifted. Something felt off about where she was sitting, like she was lower.

Isabelle tried to move her left hand and found she couldn't. When she looked over, she found it half-submerged in the rock. And it kept sinking.

"Rubarch! MATT!"

"What, what—?" Rubarch tore the headphones off, his face crumpled with irritation. It paled when he saw her hand.

It sank lower.

Isabelle whipped her head over to him. She was partially submerged, hand, back, parts of her legs, in the stone now.

"What's going on, what's—?!"

And in that moment, she fell all the way through.

-

The first thing she felt was a stiff, bumpy, almost pebbled sort of surface against her back.

Isabelle moaned and her eyes, as if disconnected by reflex or instinct or something else, began to open on their own.

A dull, buzzing white light snaked its fingers under eyelids and brought them up and open like lifting an old garage door.

She was staring at a row of fluorescent lights.

A couple dark shapes, hunched over, hooded, with big white eyes, bright as car headlights, looked down at her.

Isabelle scrambled up. She looked around.

She was in an office bullpen. The floor was that rough, economic style of carpet that so often blanketed the corporate earth. It was a mottled blue-gray-brown, a sediment at the bottom of the ocean.

In the honeycomb of cubicles sat short, foggy figures, as featureless as bedsheet ghosts, and none of them any bigger than a breakroom wastebasket. They sat at their desks, occupied by chunky beige computers twenty years out of date. Most of their monitors were the blank pale blue of the homescreen. A few looked like they were working on spreadsheets. But all of them seemed quietly aimless. Their stubby arms guided their mouses with silent, drifting movements. One, Isabelle saw, was just dragging its cursor from one end of the homescreen to the other. It seemed absorbed in the task, like it was watching a metronome, waiting for the beat to change.

A couple of the figures in the cubicles closest to Isabelle were watching her. She noticed how their colors shifted with the cloudy grace of sand kicked up under water. Their bodies tapered off, fading into almost nothing at the bottom.

One of them, a figure to her right, whose desk was decorated with a few simple, poorly-taken photos of a black-and-white housecat, waved at her. The motion was small and faint, and like everything the ghosts in the office did, silent.

Isabelle waved back.

The figure gestured again, pointing with its whole arm down the strip of carpet separating the two rows of cubicles. At the end of the strip was a brown door.

She followed the line of the point, then looked back at the figure. Its arm was still up.

She raised her arm and pointed at the door.

The figure bobbed its head in a slow up and down. Apparently satisfied, it turned back to its computer and its cat photos and resumed working.

Isabelle walked the length of the strip and reached the door.

She was about to turn the nob when she noticed, with a pause, it felt like something had shifted.

She turned around and found the entire office staring at her.

A couple of them, after a moment, waved.

She waved back.

Isabelle opened the door.

It was like she'd blinked and shown up somewhere else.

Isabelle looked around. She was in what she'd only be able to describe as some white space, somewhere.

A towering, stooped figure stared down at her. It lowered its head. The body was curved, a bent question mark, in some kind of long, matted fur cloak. The face looked almost like painted wood, the massive visage of an owl, with eyes that moved behind the eyes. But Isabelle couldn't tell what was real and what wasn't.

She stood still.

The figure shuffled around her, it's cloak swishing quietly. The smell of asphalt and grass filled her nose. Pungent but somehow whole.

After a minute, it had come back around to the front. It dipped its head a few times and extended one of the sleeves of its cloak. A massive hand, the size of a rake, with thin, bony, black-clawed fingers, came out. It looked Isabelle in the eye. It waited.

"oh."

She extended her own hand and grabbed what she could of the thing's palm. Its fingers wrapped around her own. They felt like dry tree branches. But they were warm.

It shook, and so did she.

-

Isabelle inhaled sharply and sat up. Her back was soaked, and she turned around—she'd been lying in the grass. Just a ways behind her was the small stone monument.

She rubbed her forehead, trying to clear the traces of vertigo in the front of her head and in her stomach. She'd got the feeling she'd been falling and suddenly came-to.  That had happened all the time right before she'd gone to bed as a kid.

"Hey."

Isabelle looked up.  Rubarch was leaned on the hood of his Cherokee, headphones around his neck, computer still lit up.

He set the equipment down and came over and bent down, offering her a hand.

She took it and rose, a bit unsteady.

"You alright?"

"Mhmmm."  She nodded, rubbing her eyes.  Something swelled in her chest, and there was a wetness in the back of her mouth.  She doubled over and vomited.  Rubarch rubbed her back.

"Told you, you won't forget."

She coughed and wiped her mouth.  He handed her a water bottle.  She squirted it into her mouth, swished it around, and spit.  She looked at him, handing it back.

"You knew."

He nodded.

She sighed and went back over to the stone monument.  Isabelle hesitated for a second, then thought, and sat down anyway.  Rubarch sat next to her.

"You got a good reference, though."

"What?"

He gestured to the Cherokee.  She got to her feet, and followed, and he brought her over to one of the Cherokee's side mirrors and tilted it up a bit so she could see.

Her hair was completely white.  A snowy kind of youthful.

She groaned.

"It's good luck, don't worry."

"Thanks, Matt."

"I only got this," he pointed to the birthmark under his eye. "Probably because I came back." He shrugged. "So, you definitely got lucky.  It's a great recommendation."

She leaned back against the car and exhaled.  Her arms and legs tingled.  She felt hungover, but her head was oddly clear.

"Alright," Rubarch stood. "Let's go.  We'll get your paperwork done and you can head home early, yeah?"

She looked at him for a moment.  "Could we stop for breakfast at the diner before we do?"

He looked around and shrugged.  "I don't see why not."

The two climbed into the Cherokee as the edges of the sea-green morning sky began to warm.

# CradL

Rosemary found Joe right where she'd left him the previous morning—on top of the mountain, a pale blue sky the only remnant of a fading night, the stars distant memories. A lone old tree with rough dry bark hunched after an age of solitude gave him shade in the cool sun that promised a slow warmth later in the day.

He looked half-asleep, as if he'd been waiting there almost all night—but as she came closer, his head picked up and his best wide-awake smile spread across his face.

She sat down in the grass next to him and yelped—it was wet, covered in dew. He laughed and smoothed it out with his jacket. "Sorry. I was here long enough, I should've done that earlier."

"Hopefully not too long."

"Nah."

She put her hand in his and they both sat there a while, watching as the moon faded to a ghost of itself, half in the sky, as the sun carefully inched its way up and over the mountains far away. It took its time. That was fine with her.

"So," he said. "Today's the big day."

"Our big day," Rosemary murmured.

She hadn't thought much about what today meant, not

really. She'd made her mind up a long time ago. Now that it was here, though… well, she'd never had a day like this. A genuinely new day. It was exciting. And irritating.

Joe sighed. "I wish we had a little more privacy."

"Me too," Rosemary said. "But I guess if you weren't you and I wasn't me, I wouldn't be here with you. I'd have privacy but I wouldn't have you. I'd rather have you."

She rested her head on Joe's shoulder and closed her eyes.

"Well," he said, and she was partially listening, feeling the vibrations of his voice on her cheek when he spoke. It was a simple guilty pleasure in life, she had discovered, to find a fix you never felt the urge to turn away from. "Maybe we'll get some after today."

"I'm counting on it."

She could feel his body shift as he laid his head up against the tree and exhaled. Rosemary closed her eyes. She was content. She hoped he was too.

Mom and Dad had plans. But so did she. And sitting on the mountain with Joe, Rosemary realized that no matter what happened today, no matter how she felt, this would be the moment she'd remember. The one she'd chase for the rest of her life.

—

>Happy Birthday Rosey!! :)
*Delivered at 7:03 A.M.*

Linda should have been doing work. She still had to fire off the morning update to LaMarr, which meant running full checks all across Rosemary—brainwave function, sleep cycle habits, communicative anomalies, the whole gamut CradL had drawn up to try and keep the project as steady and consistent as possible.  But how consistent, really, could they expect a teenage girl to be?

So, instead, she was scrolling through newsfeeds and waiting on a reply from her daughter.

Her cursor stopped above a video.  The thumbnail was a middle-aged anchor with a soft lantern jaw, one of the more popular public voices, in front of a dark blue map of the world.  A control room of journalists was laid out behind him.  She clicked.

"Eighteen years ago, two brilliant young scientists conceived an idea.  Almost two decades later, we, not just the United States, but all of humankind, stand on the brink of what some are calling the next foot forward in human evolution.  These words would normally belong to science fiction —today, they are real, and they lead to an unprecedented and hopeful future.

"But who are Carlos Clarke and Dr. Linda Field?  Our team has been working around the clock the past several years to put together what little information we have on the First Dad and First Mom.  Tomorrow, this network will be releasing an hour-long cable special and a tell-all book that begs, and answers, the most pressing questions: who are these two people?  What is their role in CradL?  How involved were they?  Where did they come from?  What have they done?"

Linda paused the video.  The anchor was frozen, mid-monologue.  She'd keep him that way.

The tabloid interest wasn't surprising.  But, like all

journalistic endeavors, they'd arrived at the wrong conclusions several decades too late.

The First Kids had been in the works in some form or another since the early 1980s, long before she'd arrived at CradL. Back then, and for most of its lifetime, the organization had really just been the passion project of Harold LaMarr, the garden-variety typical eccentric billionaire who so desperately wanted aliens to be real that he'd built an entire private enterprise to confirm his delusions. Like so many others of his kind, he was too blind, in Linda's opinion, to the benefit of the real. He looked to the future and hoped it would come, instead of delivering himself the present.

LaMarr had passed away five years after the First Steps. His son, Louis, had taken up his father's mantle, and along with it, the half-curated, half-authentic aloofness that allowed the man before him to accrue such wealth with so little awareness as to what he was actually doing. She knew LaMarr didn't read her reports. And, in a way, she was fine with that. Happy, even. Less fingers in the pot meant less interference in her work.

Few people understood how engineered most of what they took as real really was, and how real most of the things they mistook for being designed—intelligent, benevolent, malicious, or otherwise—really turned out to be.

For example, CradL was really a full acronym: The Center of Research for Alien/Developing Life. But "CRADL" didn't look as cool, as aesthetically pleasing, on a kid's t-shirt as "CradL" did. That's what Carlos had said. For whatever reason—Carlos knew more about it than she did, a point of contention that had spared her no prick or obstruction—

people liked "CradL" better. It was less blaring, less clinical. It looked more like something from one of the public's science fiction fantasies, a mysterious, shadowy, hopefully well-intentioned organization, other than what it really was—a small-fry private business commandeered by global scientific, military, academic, and financial interests only a couple years after its initial founding.

This was the same reason why the terminology surrounding the project's results, its subjects—the First Kids, the First Girl, the First Boy—wasn't more auspicious or grandiose. Initially, CradL's Committee had wanted to go the biblical route. Why not Adam and Eve? Call the product the Cardinal Lamb. Something more formal, something that sounded older. Carlos had been the one—he was a marketing consultant, the face of the business, Linda had no idea where the press got off calling him a scientist—to point out that people were tired of the Big being capital and unapproachable. If they were going to get people, *people* people, not academics, hobbyists, or elites, to buy into CradL, they needed to make it more relatable. They needed to use colloquialisms, they needed to pay attention to design. In other words, as Linda had gradually come to realize, they needed to dumb it down for the public.

And, much to her annoyance, it worked. The intellectual property alone had secured a global fiefdom steered by the Committee members, and their goodwill towards Carlos followed in suit. No one had ever successfully merchandised a scientific project, much less one with so little actual transparency with the public. Going to space? That was easy, that was approachable, and more importantly, that was normal.

If they could normalize the Kids, they'd not only tap a near-bottomless reservoir of public support and intrigue—they'd monopolize the science fiction market. They'd make all those little nerds' wet dreams come true.

So that's what they did.

Linda exxed out the news window and checked her messages again.

>Happy Birthday Rosey!! :)

*Delivered at 7:03 A.M.*

After eighteen years of being in her daughter's head, Linda thought that there'd be some kind of mutual understanding. But even doctorates and a responsibility to the human race couldn't break through the teenage girl's now-perennial, since she'd turned sixteen, cynicism.

Linda clicked on another window in the laptop, a pop-up black screen littered with columns of multi-colored numbers and letters. Rosemary's subroutines. Not subroutines—no, that wasn't right. Subconscious. Brainwaves showed subdued, but active, levels in the orbitofrontal cortex. She was still asleep. Probably dreaming.

Linda could edit out the cynicism if she wanted to. It'd be as easy as changing the tires on a car. But the whole point of CradL was organic synthesis. Warts and all. Whatever came out of today was whatever came out. As imperfect and unscientific as it would be.

*Unscientific.* Over the lifespan of the project, it had gone from a slur, to an excuse, to a joke, to now a selling point. A brand. Her brainchildren had become nothing more than a public spectacle, something for the audiences of various media to engorge themselves on, day-in, day-out, waiting for her and her partner to turn out today's messiah.  It was gross... but she'd resolved to let them have a circus, if that's what they wanted.  It was her success.

And it was *her* success.  Carlos never would have agreed if she hadn't persuaded him.  He'd been burned out by the project before the first steps had even been taken.  And now he was the one they all loved, even though he paraded himself in a drunken, caddie stupor all over every single front page of every major and minor publication nearly every week.  She knew he wasn't doing his job.  So she'd resigned herself to the fact that Rosemary would have to do the work of both Kids.

Linda sighed and leaned back in her chair.  Her quarters were a simple, Spartan studio.  Hardwood floors, a bed in the corner, a rudimentary kitchen complete with a sink, a drying rack—no dishwasher—and a stove, on top of which sat a chubby green teapot.  It started to whistle and Linda got up from her table, closed the laptop, went to the stove and lifted the kettle off.  She poured the steaming water into a cruddy cream coffee mug and resolved to let it steep in her hand as she went outside.

She exited her room and went down the hall, its walls an opaque velvet, a faint warmth floating from them.

She reached the end of the hall and opened the door to one of the outside balconies.

It was a porch with an iron railing.  A rusty green chair with a faded yellow cushion sat warming in the sun.  She sank into it and checked her watch.  8:14.

She looked up—far above, following Rosemary's neck, as

wide as a suspension bridge, up up up all the way to her face. Her eyes were closed. Subtle movement twitched behind the lids. Her lips were parted slightly, and soft breath came in and out in regular, slow intervals.

She remembered the day Rosemary had been born. A tiny, pink little peanut, wailing in the sterile halls of CradL's Nursery. Linda had been one of several dozen candidates. Every woman at CradL wanted to be the First Mom—but they weren't strong enough, and neither were their children. Other than Joe, Rosemary was the only one to survive the First Year. Of course, there were accusations of fallacious nepotism, that Linda wasn't just smart, but clever too, and she knew the quickest way to assure her own child's success wasn't on the grounds of merit, personal, scientific, or otherwise, but rather kneeling, asking God for one last favor.

Linda had to laugh. Let them think whatever they wanted, the reality stayed the same. They'd failed. And now, eighteen years later, she was the First Mom and they were all still where she'd left them. Bitter old women in lab coats.

Linda smiled and turned out to the place beyond the balcony. Rolling green Montana hills, stubbled with rock and trees, spread out, quilted a long time ago by divine hands. There was a town nestled in between a few of the closer hills. Linda had gone down there a few times since she and Rosemary had decided to settle for a while before the Birthday.

The doctor sank a little further in her chair, dunking the teabags in and out. She took a drink. A little too mineral, but almost immediately, she began to wake up. She looked up at her daughter again and sighed. Probably should let her sleep.

Just a little longer.  She checked her watch again.  8:17.  She'd wake Rosemary up at 8:30.

-

The inside of Joe always felt empty, but clear.

Carlos shifted, half-awake, under the thin covers of his bed.  After a few moments, he accepted, with a sigh, that sleep wasn't coming back.  He found himself staring at the ceiling, hands loosely folded on his stomach, wrapped part-ways by the blankets.

His room was a massive, open space in Joe's chest, neighbor to the heart, just one level up.  The size of a warehouse, there wasn't much in it other than Carlos' bed and the bay windows that poured in light from all times of day and night, from the front and the sides.  He never knew what to think about them.  They were nice sometimes, letting the light in, making him feel warm and almost, but not quite, at rest.  Other times, especially at night, alone in a quiet, absent son, he couldn't figure out what they made him.

Carlos was still in his clothes from the night before.  Faded slacks, a loose shirt and tie.  He'd come home early last night after trying to go out for a drink. By the third round, he'd brushed away a couple local girls and one wide-eyed hole-in-the-wall conspiracy theorist.  By the fourth round he paid and left.

The press made him out as a debauched soul who prowled the neon nights for young blood. So any time he went out, they invariably ran a story about how, once again, Carlos

Clarke hit the bricks, hungry for young women—who threw themselves at him—and looking for a good spot to drink and maybe an even better place to fight.

In reality, he was tired. He was very very tired.

He'd gotten into a few fights the first several months of the project. After that, he'd stopped drinking in public regularly. He really stopped going out at all. Most days he wandered around Joe, or he stared out the windows, or he read for however long he could. Joe had never been social. He rarely initiated any kind of conversation. And Carlos, as much as he wanted to, as much as he was good at it, couldn't find it in him to talk either.

He'd had plenty of time to think about it. He'd never had a block like this before. But the thing was, it wasn't a block necessarily—a block occurred when you wanted to do something, when you needed to do it so bad, you'd find a way around whatever was obstructing the path forward, and you'd keep going.

But Carlos didn't want to talk with Joe. He didn't know why. It was a blank, open, empty feeling. And even after almost twenty years, it was still new. He didn't hate his son, he didn't pity him, he didn't not care for him, or not want him to succeed... but there just wasn't anything there. They were two people, living in the same place, who existed around each other.

At first, he'd tried to rationalize it. He wanted to convince himself it was really because of Linda. She'd lied to him. Gotten him to come with her, spend that night, and that's what had landed him here.

But after a few years, the motivation ran out from that line, and he found he didn't really feel much anger towards her at all. He'd wanted to be there. He'd made the choice to see her. And now he was here. That's where life led you. That was how it worked.

So eventually he'd landed on the idea that him and Joe were just different people. Regardless of blood relation or intimacy, they were simply different. Not so different they couldn't co-exist, but different enough where the gap between was too large and too foreign for either to surmount without the effort feeling oddly artificial towards the other.

And so Carlos found himself staring at the ceiling, a headache beginning to brew from the previous night. He'd opened up a bottle in his study when he'd gotten back and polished most of it off before midnight.

He got out of bed and stretched, massaging the back of his neck. The inside of his mouth was dry, and his tongue stuck a bit to the roof, and the backs of his teeth. He rubbed his face, walking across the room as morning light began to drift in, heading towards the stairwell that led to his study.

In a way, he thought, heading carefully down the cement stairs winding down towards his study, each level fitted with a stern, tall window, this was the longest time he'd ever been alone, by his own choice. He'd sequestered himself to Joe after a few years of trying to live in the public eye. He couldn't handle people anymore, which was what he'd built his entire life around. He'd always been able to schmooze, to talk with anyone, to walk into a room and, if not run it, then run the conversation.

But he got in his own way. People didn't want to talk to him now. They wanted to talk to Carlos Clarke, P.R. rockstar, a man of the night. This guy who just didn't exist.

He hung by one of the staircase windows for a moment and looked out. They'd stopped in a small Western town, somewhere in Idaho, maybe, if Carlos remembered correctly. It was huge, spread-out, billowing and old green.

Carlos moved on, reached the bottom of the stairs, and quietly headed into his office, a cluttered shrine with posters and merchandise decorating the walls and shelves. There was an over-the-hill coffee pot on the bookshelf, half-full from last night. Next to it, an old CradL coffee mug, unwashed. He poured the cold coffee and sat down at his desk, where a single chunky monitor blinked the CradL logo at him. The bottle from last night was still there, and his glass had tipped over. With a delicate unease in his stomach, he took both, opened the bottom drawer of his desk, and laid them to rest with a careful clink. He stretched up and leaned back, queuing up a random video from his personal hard drive.

It was bygone promotional reel they'd put together ten years ago to inform the public, as well as soothe fears and expectations, regarding CradL. The graphics were done in what had been the style of the day. Smooth, colorful, chipperly-edited animations that looked part modern art propaganda and part game cutscene. A young woman's voice, with the tenor of professionalism and a cultivated slightly-contained-but-palpable excitement, explained over the course of the video what people could expect from CradL in the coming decade.

Carlos had been the director. He'd written most of the

script. He'd been alongside this promotional bit every step of the way. And now it wasn't anything but ancient, optimistic, naïve history.

He stood by his decisions, his choices, and what he'd admittedly influenced the public into choosing, seeing, and believing. CradL wasn't just one of the most radical and novel scientific endeavors in the history of the species—it was also, under his watch, one of the most concerted and beautifully-woven marriages of science and public relations—propaganda, his critics had claimed—ever exercised in such scope and scale.

There was no practical reason that the Kids had to be ten stories tall, half-naked, conventionally attractive, and so on. Organic synthesis, at least Linda's postulation of it, could easily be achieved by constructing two massive organic brains, augmented and updated by modern technology and cybernetics, wired into the collective history and continual self-generating cycle of human discourse that persisted every day across and in every corner of the web. Of course, in order to truly be able to not only process, but synthesize all that information, the brains had to be huge. Literally massive— hence the Kids' size.

But what was likeable, or alluring, or grand, or most impor- tantly, *human*, about two gigantic cybernetic brains in jars? Would that test well with any demographic outside the closets of hardline academics, scientists, and fringe enthusiasts?

Studies said, no, and so did Carlos, because he'd read the studies and written more than a few of them. That was why he had completely re-oriented and restructured the project. The Kids had to be people, human beings, at least in form and fundamental function. They'd still need to be massive for the sake of computing and synthetic power, but every action necessary would need to be taken in order to give them humanity. They couldn't just be freakshow science projects—the public had to be able to *see themselves* in the project. They had to feel like they were a part of the story; and they were, in all reality. The results of CradL, true organic synthesis between two human beings, birthing a new knowledge and understanding, creating a messianic bridge between all humankind through science and human nature... well, of course that would affect them. It would change everything. But that change wasn't sexy 99% of the time, especially if it happened behind closed doors, if the scientists and leaders behind the initiative were kept out of the public eye. That's when rumors started sprouting up like mushrooms in the dank, dark shadows created by needless secrecy. It was better, in Carlos' opinion, to let the public in as much as they could. It followed the same principle that governed television—people had no influence over the sitcom couples they watched year after year, yet felt so strongly attached and connected to them. Most of them had no idea how the shows they loved got made; all they knew was that, for some reason, they cared. That investment had to be generated by the Kids. And, if possible, by the two people directly responsible for them.

Linda, of course, didn't agree, and Carlos couldn't blame her. She was a scientist through and through, a child of rationality, empiricism, reason. He was the opposite—if you believed the news.

He sat back in his chair and sipped his coffee. A message from Joe scrolled up along his screen.

>late night?

*Delivered at 9:02 A.M.*

*Seen at 9:02 A.M.*


Carlos nodded. Joe wasn't dumb. He could monitor Carlos' vital signs, his brain functions, and even, within a small margin of error, predict rough patterns of behavior. Much like a son would come to know his father's habits and pitfalls. The only difference was that Joe was often incredibly accurate, and therefore rarely wrong, and nearly impossible to lie to. At least, in that way, the Kid made him more honest. A bit better. And he had to be thankful for that.

>celebrating your birthday a bit early. We're gonna get moving soon, u wanna do/see anything before we go?

*Delivered at 9:03 A.M.*

*Seen at 9:03 A.M.*

...

...

...


>I want to get there first.

*Delivered at 9:04 A.M.*

*Seen at 9:04 A.M.*


Carlos actually laughed out loud. The Kid was competitive, that had been his nature since he'd been born. But he was also sentimental.  So this impulse... ah, he was probably just excited.

>Then let's get a move-on.  And happy birthday!!

*Delivered at 9:05 A.M.*

*Seen at 9:05 A.M.*

...

...

>Thanks dad.

*Delivered at 9:06 A.M.*

*Seen at 9:06 A.M.*

Carlos began to make the requisite calls, and some last-minute messages were shot off to local, state, federal, and CradL authorities.  Any time the Kids moved, everyone had to know.  Partially for safety, and partially because everyone wanted some time to set up chairs and watch if they could. Like a big parade going by.

-

Linda was tending her garden when her phone buzzed. She kept a whole wealth of herbs, spices, vegetables, and fruits growing in a small, naturally-lit room in Rosemary's back, right behind the third level of her ribs.  LaMarr had suggested that she and Carlos each find some ways to both occupy their time and educate their children as they got older.  Even if Rosemary's face couldn't see her, the girl was able to watch through a network of cameras and lenses that were laid across her body in an all-watching synthetic nervous system. It wasn't entirely effective, and certain things got lost in translation. The girl could talk, but rarely ever did, at least now. When she'd been a little girl and about the size of a regular little girl, Linda had been able to facilitate actual conversations with her from the outside. She'd even been able to take her around towns, to restaurants, theaters, libraries, and show her what the world looked like. Now, though, complex conversation was too slow for Rosemary, and it took too much effort to work her mouth and ears at the same time. She was a big girl, after all, and even with all the augmentations—maybe because of them—natural methods of talk were beyond her scope.

Linda checked her phone.

>Happy Birthday Rosey!! :)

*Delivered at 7:03 A.M.*

*Seen at 9:28 A.M.*

....

....

>thanks

*Delivered at 9:28 A.M.*

*Seen at 9:28 A.M.*


She began typing... and stopped. She sighed. Normally, she'd chalk a one-word-response up to adolescent curtness, but today... the girl had a lot on her mind.

Linda wiped her forehead with a rolled-up sleeve and headed out from the greenhouse. She needed to talk with Carlos about today's plans.

-

"No, yeah, it's a big day. Mhmm, I'm excited too. Yes. Alright. Thank you, mhmm. Bye Louis."

Carlos set his phone down and popped another three Ibuprofen. He rested his head on his desk with a groan. That was one thing he wouldn't miss, having to verify and triple-verify with someone every time he went somewhere with Joe.

His computer pinged. He looked up. The blocky terminal screen flickered in the dull, low light. A single message.

>Where are we meeting?

*Delivered at 9:31 A.M.*

*Seen at 9:31 A.M.*

Seeing her writing got his pulse racing at a pace that bordered on embarrassing. After all the years, and after the separation.... he missed her.

He sat up and typed, quick, rapid, but measured.

>Joe and I found this lake in the north. Can send you location. Meet there by two?

*Delivered at 9:31 A.M.*

He looked over his message just once and sent it.

It wasn't often, he had found, you got lucky enough to

meet someone like Linda. Someone who reminded you on the daily that there were still surprises you could never plan for in another person. Those were two things the news coverage had gotten wrong about them—he'd known Linda for much longer, way before CradL. And despite her appearance, she was never, ever boring.

Another ping.

>okay

*Delivered at 9:33 A.M.*

*Seen at 9:33 A.M.*

Carl's hands hovered over the keyboard, but he thought better and stopped himself from typing anymore. He knew that it wouldn't do any good, to press her. He'd just have to wait.

-

Rosemary had sat down, cross-legged, on the shore of the lake. Dark blue-black water lapped at her toes.

Linda had sat next to her. She looked up at her daughter. The girl's eyes blinked laconically. She was watching a point on the horizon. Linda couldn't tell which.

She'd realized, as Rosemary got closer to the destination, exactly where they were going. Carlos' family had an old summer retreat in the mountains. He'd taken her there once, for their honeymoon. And she'd taken him there once as well, to reconnect.

He hadn't had any idea. He'd thought it was simply a

failed love, long lost, who'd brought him out to a sentimental spot to rekindle what they'd once had. To turn over a new leaf. Her own cynicism embarrassed her almost two decades removed, and brought with it an uneasy feeling in the pit of her stomach at returning to the place.

Joe appeared over the mountains.

-

Carlos shut the cabin door. He turned around.

Linda was turning on the radio. Her hair had started to unwind out of her bun. Her sleeves were rolled up. She still looked so professional. Older. But not tired at all.

Soft electronic jazz crackled out. Linda turned around. She smiled, but her eyes were flat. "You look better."

Carlos rubbed the back of his neck. "I shaved."

Linda took a seat at the table. Orange afternoon light filtered in. Carlos sat across from her. She poured a glass of wine, first for him, then for her. Carlos sipped it. In a few moments the whole glass was gone. Linda raised an eyebrow. Carlos sighed.

"I'm sorry. Old habits."

She passed him the bottle. He reached for it and poured another.

Outside the window, two small black silhouettes sat on top of the mountain. He could tell, even from here, one was inclined to the other. They were talking. About what, he had no idea.

"Eighteen years." Linda didn't look at him. He rubbed his chin.

"Flew by."

Linda shrugged.  The lines on her forehead had darkened and thinned in the past couple decades.  She never went on T.V..  Not out of vanity.  More out of spite.  It worked.  The press loved her "mysterious woman" persona.  Carlos was the more entertaining of the two; Linda was the more interesting.

"What now?"

Linda tipped her glass back.  It looked like she barely drank anything.  "Let's hope they like each other."

Carlos raised his glass.  "Cheers to that."

She eyed him for a moment before tipping her glass to his.  A soft clink joined them in the cabin.

-

The alarm she'd set hadn't gone off—instead, Linda was woken up by a cool morning breeze filtering in through the windows, brushing her hair back and lightly touching her cheeks.  It tumbled through the windows with the scent of the mountains hitchhiking on its back.

She sat up in bed, pulling the covers along up with her.  A weight stopped them midway through, and she looked.

Carlos, sleeping peacefully, little breaths coming in and out through parted lips.  She remembered, that's almost exactly how he'd looked eighteen years ago.  There was a moment of tenderness she felt, a little pang in her chest.  She brushed his hair back.  All the things she'd thought about him, eighteen years of constructing who he was in her mind, from memories that had faded as the Kids had grown... and now, here they were again. Here she was again. Next to a man who she'd found harder and harder, supposedly, to respect, waking up late in a bed together.

Linda bent down over the edge of the bed and groped for a familiar, an old familiar, feeling of balled-up underwear and her undershirt. She slipped her bottoms on and pulled the shirt over her head. It smelled like wine, smoke, and Carlos' cologne.

She looked back at the sleeping man, sprawled out on the bed like an oversized kid. He was so... honest. Too honest. Too open. There was something about him, the way he walked and carried himself, like he'd never been stopped in his life, ever.

He was a bit different now—he seemed more tired. Slower. But even then, there was still a sense that he knew just where he was going and what he was doing. Even if he was wrong, and he oftentimes was, he'd bounce back, having taken an unexpected detour, and continue on his way.

She wished she could be like that. One, she couldn't see the utility in that kind of open-bookness, at least, not all the time, not in the universal manner Carlos applied to it.

Second, she loved her work. Carlos was always separate from what he did. It didn't embody him, heart, soul, and all the rest. For her... well. She'd never found stability in the companionship of others. Not him. Or her family. Friends. Even the Kids. What she did find stable, what made sense to her, was the work she did. No matter who left, died, broke-up, abandoned, or said bye-bye forever, she could always go back to her desk at the end of the day, no matter where that desk was, and find her work, waiting for her, like a cat reposing with half-lidded eyes and a flicking tail. Her work was her. It was alive. More alive than she found most people to be, at least.

Linda padded her way out the door and into the kitchen. She put on a tea-kettle for herself and a pot of coffee for Carlos.

She looked out the window. The two figures, Joe and Rosemary, were gone. Probably laying down behind the mesa somewhere. Maybe they were sleeping. Or talking. About all the futures that lay ahead.

The clock on the stove, she noted, read 9:17. She had a sudden urge—partially panic from the absence of the Kids, and partially an excitement to hold the results of an eighteen-year experiment in her arms—to wake Carlos up, get him dressed, and truck up and down the mountain in the old jalopy that rested like a beaten-up workhorse under the flimsy wood-plank addition that made up the garage at the cabin.

But she didn't do that. Instead, she sat at the table, waiting for the kettle to boil over. For the first time in nearly two decades, she had nothing to do. No one that had to be talked to. No lessons to give. No checks to run. In fact, by noon at the latest that day, her contract with CradL would be terminated. Of course, there'd be an opportunity for a re-up—and she'd take it. She'd earned it. But as of the moment, she was in the bleak, uncertain, and yet promising and exciting edge of her known territory. Of everything she'd done, not just for CradL, but long before that. It felt, as clichéd as it was, and if she said it out loud Carlos would never, ever let her hear the end of it, like the book had been closed. Not just the turning of a page or the conclusion of a large and impressive chapter.

Rather, now, she was done with that volume of her life.  Even when she went back to CradL, she wouldn't be the same girl who left it eighteen years ago with some dinky ex of hers she'd conned—encouraged sounded better but conned was more accurate, if she was being honest—into assisting her.

The tea kettle began to whistle, and she made her way to the stove and carefully lifted it off.  She noticed, subtly, but it was there—she was quieter.  A bit more careful and cautious.  Well, of course.  She didn't want to wake Carlos up.  And there was that wry, if a bit melancholic, grin in her soul, a voice in the echoes of her mother, "My goodness, Linda. How soft."  She could feel her mother brushing her hair and whispering words to the same dry, but supportive, effect.

Linda sat back down at the table, her mug steaming, and absentmindedly dunked the teabags in and out while she looked out the window.  And it hit her, in that moment.  The work was done.

Someone wrapped their arms around her and she heard a sleep-coated, scratchy voice say, "Thinking about big things this early?"

"Mhmmm," she nodded into the arms.

He kissed her on the forehead, a muffled sucker, and moved past her to the coffee pot.  "No way!" he grabbed the bag of grounds, the same kind they'd had when they'd been living together.  He turned around and looked like a kid who'd just been kissed.  "You remembered?"

"Guess I did," she smiled at him.

It was around 10:30 when they'd both showered, cleaned up, and had a light breakfast. Linda had insisted she wasn't hungry, but Carlos had made a small plate of bacon and eggs anyway. For himself, he assured, she didn't have to eat anything if she really wasn't hungry. She nibbled on a bit of the bacon and had half a sunny-side up egg. She hadn't had breakfast like that in ages.

They headed out the door and made for the old jalopy out behind the cabin, one they'd bought from the town half an hour away. They'd used to rumble up and down the mountain in it, looking for and finding good picnic spots. They both climbed in the jalopy, Linda driving and Carlos riding shotgun, and tumbled off and up into the mountains. There weren't any windows in the vehicle, just a crude latticework, a thick frame that Carlos held on to with a bit of a queasy expression—one of the reasons Linda hadn't eaten much. She smiled a bit and hoped he'd be okay.

The air grew colder and sharper. It felt as blue as the cloudless morning sky above them. Everything above seemed so close and so clear, the mountain a rolling mass of brown and green, a mysterious watcher, a natural god, put on and in the earth to remind human beings of their scope. To humble them. Linda supposed that could be one interpretation. Or it was a randomly-formed mass of stone and rock resulting from millions of years of gradual tectonic shifts. Did the science behind it demystify the mountain? Did it have to? Could you explain God and still believe in him?

She wrenched the wheel one more time, hard to the right, then to the left, the beaten tires acting like hooves, carefully plodding their way up a steep, treacherous pass not often taken. With a final lurch, the jalopy heaved itself up onto the flat terrace, a little field, gradually sloped, an unfurling prodigal mountain branching from its mother.

And it was here, for the first time since high school, Linda felt that kind of fear so surprising in its intensity and so sudden in its appearance that it was almost like a death.

The flat hillock's grass had been dug into, torn up, flattened, like there'd been a colossal match between two gods the night before. And, in a way, there had.

So where were they?

Linda got out of the Jeep. Her heart hammered her ribs and vibrated her throat. She felt sick. She barely registered the passenger side door slamming shut, and Carlos making his way around and sitting on the hood.

"Any idea where they might have gone?"

Linda shook her head. "They weren't supposed to go anywhere. They were supposed to stay right here."

A rough chuckle scratched from his throat. Hands thrust in his pockets, he walked across the grass, head swinging this way and that. In his blocky black Ray Bans, Hawaiian Shirt, and flat, dirty sneakers, he looked every bit the slacker superstar the press had made him out to be. A tourist in the world and its people.

She walked through the grass. There was a heavy, hot scent inundating, a lingering phantasm of the past night's exploits. One of the greatest midnight beasts humankind would ever know. And now it was gone. Vanished.

"Hey."

She looked up. Carlos was staring at something, near the

edge of the field.  He'd bent down, his head craned, like he was tracking something.

Linda came over and saw exactly what he did.

Two pairs of footprints, dug into the mountain, heading down the slope, then out across the plains.  She cupped her hands over her eyes and tried to follow the trail.  But it looked like it ended a few miles or so from where it began.  There wasn't anything other than a large half-mile scorch mark.

"Looks like they flew the coop," Carlos stood up, dusting off his hands.  "I didn't know they could do that."

"It was a precautionary measure," Linda said, her voice trailing, spooling off into thought.  "They weren't supposed to be able to use it unless they thought they were in mortal danger."

"Ouch," Carlos sucked through his teeth.  "Not a great review, huh?"

Linda knew he was joking, but her chest felt like a part of it had literally been scooped up and thrown halfway across the valley.  She fell back on her ass with an involuntary give-out that surprised even her, and watched as a few stray clouds and their shadows ambled over the grass beyond.

A lifetime of work.  Gone.  Her eyes stung and something sharp and hot bit in her nose.  She sniffed.

Carlos sat down next to her.  She couldn't look at him.

"So," he said after a long moment.  "We're out of a job?"

She nodded.

"Any way we could find them?"

She shook her head.

"Any idea where they might've gone?"

She shook her head.

He leaned back, palms in the grass, head tilted up towards the sky. They sat like that for a while. And then he leaned forward.

"You know, I found this great fishing spot a few years back. Really remote. Up in the Yukon. There's a cute little cabin, a cruddy Jeep, and a fully-stocked wet bar. I was waiting until everything was all over to take a little vacation up there."

She looked over at him. He was looking at her, a half-smile on his face. He tilted his glasses down the bridge of his nose, and his eyes swept side-to-side, conspicuously covert. "Do you know anyone else who might need a little time off?"

In that moment, despite it all, Linda snorted. Seeing his smile grow, she rolled her eyes and stood up. "I might. She's really a bum, though."

"Eh," Carlos waved his hand, standing up, and put an arm around her shoulder. "That means she's probably a quick packer. All the better."

Linda walked back with him to the Jeep, her arm around him, and listened to him talk. For the first time in her life, she had nothing, not even her work, to fall back on. She looked up at him, still making talk, joking, trying to get her to laugh, with all the enthusiasm of a recent high school graduate bound for bigger and better things, and she realized that in twenty years, nothing had really changed. And she smiled.

In the Castle
of the Summer Age

EXECUTIVE ORDER 21A
THE WORLD INTERIOR DEP.
A FORMAL NOTICE

Dear All,

I'll keep this brief.

All official documentation regarding the Reformation will be attached, along with this letter. This is merely a forward sketch of the intentions further broken down into detail throughout the subsequent documents.

As of January 1$^{st}$, all national intelligence agencies are hereby dissolved, as per the October Sentence carried unanimously by the Interior Council and all 198 national signatories. All former intelligence personnel must report to their Relocation Officers by no later than January 30$^{th}$; failure to do so will enact Article 4(b) of the Interior Code of Human Rights. For any intelligence official who fails to report to their regional Relocation Office by no later than a week past January 30$^{th}$, Interior Officers will have full discretion under the New Laws to detain or neutralize the former intelligence personnel.

The personnel who comply will receive a 1/7$^{th}$ lifetime pension. This has been reduced from the previous 1/4$^{th}$ pension discussed in September, after further review during the October Sentence brought forth crimes against humankind and gross violations of human rights of which the Council had heretofore been unaware.

All former personnel will be relocated within two months of their appointment. Their location, identity, and person will be kept unavailable from all records—local, regional, national, and international—except those filed with the Interior.

All former personnel who have been sentenced to relocation will remain at their designated site until further action is taken either with their own individual case, or with the case of their agency as a whole (see Central Intelligence Agency Case File, active, in document 32b).

Violation of the personnel's relocation will warrant immediate Interior action. All violators will be treated as hostile.

The Interior regards this matter and all those involved as one of the most serious cases of mass crimes against humankind in history. Though not all those involved in intelligence operations throughout the Old World may have been fully aware of the extent of their actions, they were, regardless of intention, complicit in operations that endangered the lives of millions and forever damaged millions more. As such, all have been found guilty. There is no recourse for this decision. There is no appeal. It will stand until death.

On the next page you will find the names of all those sentenced to death as per the October Sentence. Each National Notary Representative must sign for their country's personnel.

Thank you for your cooperation. The Interior humbly accepts the mantle of supra-national responsibility for all peoples in this New World.

We look forward to standing side-by-side with you in a better future.


Sincerely,

Johannes Fosburg

Secretary General of the World Interior

Chapter One

The Castle on the Cliff

The old gunmetal green Daytona sped down the coastal dirt road, kicking up earth and grit in pale clouds as it thundered on the edge of the Atlantic.  A cool wind tugged at the moss-brown jacket and hair of the figure leaning back on the seat as it took a detour, a left, at a fork in the road, towards a wooded path.

It whirred down an aisle of birch and oak trees, a canopy of ochre and amber and orange shivering and quietly snowing their leaves, one by one.

After a minute or so the bike emerged on the other side of the wood to a small open field of dry green grass.  A lone lighthouse stood at the other end of the field, on the precipice of the cliffs, a century-old citadel of cream brick and stone.  Grey clouds passed overhead in a silent current as the rider came to a stop just twenty feet from the lighthouse.

He kicked the stand up and sat for a moment on the bike before dismounting, running his hands through his hair before taking out a crushed softpack of Madoff cigarettes, cupping his hands and lighting one.

There was a click and the rider looked up. Ten feet, give or take, from where he stood, an old chunky Bolex camera sat on a thick tripod.

"Ah shit."

He stuffed his hands in his pockets and walked over to the camera. He checked the counter. It was at zero. He was out of film.

"Ah *shit*."

Artie Doon flicked his cigarette on the ground and snubbed it with the toe of his shoe. He went back to his bike and guided it by the handlebars to a small shed hunkered to the lighthouse's right, wheeled the Daytona in, and closed the doors. After lowering the rusted single latch that served as his only security for one of his only possessions, he dusted his hands, headed back to the camera, folded up the tripod legs, and carried the whole piece inside.

-

Muffled waves crashed against the cliffs outside the lighthouse walls as Artie pushed his way through the front door and into his living area, a wide half-circle with a tweed couch, a small brown armchair, a busted, blocky CRT T.V., a framed *Jaws* poster, and a modest kitchen spot, sat the way he'd left it the previous morning. Cigarette cartons, some empty, some not, laid around like cats. A DVD menu rested half-faint on the screen for *Escape From New York*. The theme bubbled from the television, low, the only noise other than himself in the lighthouse.

He set the camera and tripod against his couch and went

to the cupboard under the sink, pulled out a dented blue tea kettle, filled it with water from the faucet, and set it on one of the gas stove burners. He flicked it to a three before going back over to his couch and thumping down.

In a few minutes, the kettle whistled. He grabbed a grey tin cup from one of the cupboards near the stove, scooped a few grounds into it from a bag under the sink, mixed it gingerly with his pointer finger, yelped quietly, and drew it out. He sucked on it for a moment before dipping it back in, giving the coffee a few more twirls, and went back to the couch.

Artie sat there for a while, nursing his coffee. He figured he could change out the film, try to get the shot again... but what would be the point. The light would be different, and he already had upwards of ten takes of the same exact shot. He wasn't a perfectionist. He just didn't know where to go from there.

So, after ten minutes of sitting on the couch and alternating between staring blankly at the opposite wall and the television screen, Artie set his coffee down and went up the cramped, winding staircase to his room.

It wasn't much—barely big enough for his bed with a single quilt blanket and a ratty pillow near a bullet-shaped window with cloudy glass. Across from the bed was a three-drawer dresser with a mirror, a few books, and a scuffed tough maroon and cotton-white plastic tacklebox. A crude wooden fishing pole, nothing more than a shoot of cane with twine threaded down its length and a hook on the end, leaned itself up against the dresser.

Artie snagged the rod and scooped the tacklebox from the dresser top, catching a look at himself in the mirror.

He rubbed his face. A week's worth of black-grey stubble coated his jaw and cheeks. His dark hair, which had been in a sharp crew cut for most of his life, had gotten shaggy in the past few months. He had no intention of trying to cut it any time soon. He was only thirty-two. He felt dead enough to be older.

Before he left, he grabbed one of the books from the small pile on the dresser and stood in the room for a moment, thinking if he'd forgotten anything. When he remembered he didn't have much to forget, he headed down the stairs, the tacklebox jangling as he did.

He grabbed his coffee and went out the front door, taking care to lock it before walking north along a small dirt road, an offshoot of the one he'd rode down earlier, that wound up and down the coast.

Artie sipped his coffee as he walked along the path, whistling the theme from last night's movie.

About a quarter mile from the lighthouse, there was a lone, flat rock that sat on the edge of the cliffs. Artie made his way over and sat down. It was still cold and wet with morning dew and seaspray. He didn't mind.

Over the next few minutes, he carefully tied a simple plastic lure—a green rubber minnow with a red underbelly and faint brown spots—to the end of the twine.

He cast out over the edge of the cliff.

Artie set his rod down and waited. He took a book out of his jacket, some old Western. There was a sticker on the cover that read WATERSPELL LIBRARY. Most of it had been eaten away, and the letters were faded. He only knew what it said because he'd had it long before age had gotten ahold.

He sipped his coffee. The sun began to rise over the wavering horizon of the Atlantic.

After half an hour, there was a tug on the rod. Artie set down his book, took another sip of coffee, and jerked once. The weight on the end suddenly vanished. He sighed.

He pulled the twine up and checked. The lure was gone.

He fixed another one on and cast out again.

Artie pulled out a pack of Madoffs from inside his coat, slid one in his mouth, and lit it. He had to set the rod down on the rock and cup his hands to keep the tiny, jigging flame from his lighter from sputtering out. After a few unsuccessful tries, he lit, inhaled, and breathed out a cloud of blue-white smoke. He picked the rod back up and waited.

An hour later, the tip jerked. Artie flicked up—the weight on the end didn't disappear. He began to slowly, carefully, pull in the twine.

Five minutes later, he had a nice, fat WiAnno Trout.

Artie reeled it in, slung the rod and the heaving fish over his shoulder, and trekked back to Salsbury Point.

It took about an hour for Artie to clean and fry the fish, shower, and get dressed. By eleven that morning, he was heading back out his door, down the dirt road that led into the trees beyond. He'd changed into a shabby powder blue sportscoat, simple matching slacks, a salmon Hawaiian shirt underneath, and brown loafers. He carried a plain, small, thick red and white plastic cooler in one hand.

As he walked down the road, he took out a Madoff and

puffed. It was early Fall, but on the Northeast Coast, that meant next to nothing. The warmest part of the day was still to come—between one and three—and even in the short time he'd lived at Salsbury, Artie knew that he'd be lucky if, even in the Summer, the temperature got above seventy. That was the thing about his spot's ocean view—pretty enough to live there forever, cold enough to make him wonder why anyone would.

He supposed, walking down the cluster of trees that lined the road, he should have been nervous. If anyone knew he left the property, he'd have a bullet in his head before next breakfast. That was the thing, too—those Interior guys were quick, and they were cold, but at least they had the courtesy to give you peace of mind. No Wild West quick-draw bullshit, no long interrogation, none of that Old World COINTELPRO crap. You'd go to bed one night and that'd be it. You'd, quite literally, never know.

Artie admired the style. He just wished they sang a different tune with it.

He reached another path, this one cutting right into the woods off the road. He took it.

Walking through the trees, it was even quieter than on the road. The only other sound was the waving whoosh of the wind through the pine needles. It was a grey day overhead, one of those where everything seemed still, and calm. Artie imagined it would be what purgatory felt like.

The path wound on for half a mile before he came to the terminal point—an old torii gate. Its red was chalky from years of wear, and some of the wood had begun to splinter through even the more resilient coats of paint. An old man getting older as he stood watch.

Beyond the gate was a simple shrine. A bygone pagoda-type structure, with some kind of offering spot in the center. Artie had never really been so into the culture that he knew all the specifics, and no one was gonna tell him now. Regardless, he recognized it as a sacred, quiet space. And visiting gave him peace of mind and something to do.

He reached the steps and did a sort of half-bow, and after that, a sign of the cross. He wasn't practicing in either tradition, but he also figured that maybe, on the off-chance both were real, the spirits or whatever from each would get to hang out in a place like this. And if they did, he doubled his chances at any kind of help if he tried both ways. He figured that was a kind of honest desperation ghosts of all stripes and kinds might be able to respect, or at least understand. It wasn't smart, but most rituals, and the emotions that comforted them, weren't traditionally smart. They didn't have to be—that wasn't the point.

Artie came up the steps and into the pagoda. He knelt, and set the cooler down.

He folded his hands and said a short prayer.

"Dear... whoever... is out there.

It's me.

Artie.

I know you probably know that, but maybe you forget, I don't know.

I brought you fish. Again.

I know that's kinda, you know, uh, the same thing I've

brought the last few... months. But if you get sick, just send me a sign. Trust me, I'm sick of fish too."

He opened the cooler and took out the fish. He'd filleted it, and deep-fried it, and added a few French fries on the side. There was a whole jumbo frozen pack he'd stored in his freezer from the grocery run they'd let him make right before relocation. Artie wouldn't get another one for five months.

Next to the plate, he put little cups of ketchup, mayonnaise, hot sauce, and tartar sauce. He folded his hands again and sighed.

"Anyway. So. There you go.

I hope you guys, whoever you are, are doing, you know, well. And if you've been helping me, but I haven't seen it, I wanna say, uh, sorry. I'll try to keep a lookout.

If you haven't been helping, that's fine. I bet you're pretty busy.

I mean, even if you're not, and you don't, I'd like to think you can still hear me.

And so I bet you guys know it can get pretty lonely out here.

So. I'm thankful. For the company.

Even if you might just be in my head.

But. Uh. Anyway. Amen." Artie curled forward in a little half-bow, did the sign of the cross, opened his eyes, and stood up.

He picked up the cooler and walked down the stairs, turning one last time to bow. And then he left.

That night, a storm hit Salsbury Point. Artie had seen, coming back from the shrine, the grey sky beginning to lose a bit of its light, and off in the distance over the bay, a front of rolling thunderheads, grumbling to each other and anyone that'd listen.

The lighthouse had stood on the point for close to two hundred years, built from strong and sturdy stone, but he'd closed all the windows and locked the doors anyway when he'd gotten inside, just as a precaution. The wind roared outside and rain rattled the roof and pounded the stone, but the walls and doors muffled it so much that the storm in all its entirety and fury sounded miles away.

Artie dipped into the fridge and had some of the WiAnno he'd caught.

He fell asleep that night in front of the T.V.. *A Hard Day's Night* flickered across his slumped, sleeping face.

-

Something crashed outside—Artie woke up with a start. His plate clattered to the floor. He rubbed his eyes and listened.

The storm was still wailing. Whatever had made the noise could've been thunder, or lighting, or even a nearby tree from the woods falling over. If that's what it'd been, that would be a big tree.

Artie sat up for a moment. Nothing but the rain and wind made a sound.

He slowly fell back on the couch and closed his eyes.

And then there was a pounding on his door.

That, more than the crash, woke him up, fully up, really up. He got to his feet and rubbed his face. He waited.

Someone, or something, pounded on the door again. Whoever or whatever they were, they sounded small, but oddly strong.

His stomach sank. There weren't any wild animals out here, none that'd ever make this kind of noise, this late at night, during a storm like this one. And very, very few people knew who he was anymore, or where he was. And of the people who knew, he never wanted to see them again. That'd just mean more bad news.

Another round of pounding.

Artie crept over to the kitchen and pulled the knife he'd used to clean the fish from the cutting board. He didn't have any formal combat training, no experience with this kind of stuff whatsoever. He didn't even really want to fight whoever was on the other side of the door. But he wasn't going to open up his door and wait for whoever to do whatever they were gonna do. At the very least, he'd want them to know that the guy who they caught unaware watching *A Hard Day's Night* wasn't totally unprepared. Or at least, not totally resigned to his own fate.

Another thought occurred as he approached the door. The pounding continued again, a bit more furious in the beginning, and a bit softer at the end

People from the Interior would've just put a bullet through his brain, or maybe used one of their pet science project MKUltra kids to give him an aneurysm or splatter him against a wall. So unless they were doing some kind courtesy call, unless they'd changed their tune, whoever this was might not be one of them.

He was half a foot from the door when the pounding stopped.

Artie came closer.

And the door slammed open—the bolt flew wild and caught Artie in the cheek.  He cried out and cupped his face.

He looked up.

In the doorway was a young girl.  She was soaked from head to toe, wearing some old t-shirt, high waisted shorts, and ratty, soggy black Vans.  She wore a wide-brimmed black hat with a floppy, pointed top.  Her face was girlish, but Artie saw a cold age, a sharpness, behind her eyes.

She looked up and he met her gaze.  She looked exhausted, half-dead.

Something broke across her face.

Her lips parted. "...you."

And she crumpled to the ground.

Chapter Two

Alumnus

Artie leaned back on the sink. Through the window, the rosy-orange clouds of a new day looked especially fresh, coming out of last night's storm. He lit a Madoff.

The girl had been unconscious since last night. He'd watched her for a few minutes, with the rain and wind howling through the door, drops spattering the rough hardwood floor. He had no idea what to do—but eventually, after some deliberation, he'd picked her up, and set her on the couch. He'd dried her off, gingerly, with a towel, tense, waiting for her to wake up at any moment, a wild animal that'd take a chunk out of him if it came-to.

After that, Artie'd gotten a blanket and laid it over her. She was breathing slow, but regularly.

He'd watched her all night from the kitchen. The fish-cleaning knife was on the counter next to him. He felt guilty about that.

She'd recognized him. He sighed and rubbed his forehead. He'd recognized her too. He knew who she was.

He looked over at the old cramped clock fixed on the head of the stove—6:49.

A small, muffled groan made him whip his head around. He looked. She was starting to wake up.

Artie made a grab for the fish-cleaning knife…. And then he stopped, and set it down. He sighed. She was practically a kid, barely more than a teenager. She'd come from Waterspell, and he knew, roughly, what she was capable of. There was a quick, fleeting sense, a voice in the back of his head that told him not to take any chances. But he ignored it.

She sat up with a start. He watched as she carefully scanned the room, her chest rising and falling rapidly. She turned around and saw him, standing in the kitchen. He tensed.

And then she groaned and fell back.

"Oh my God," she laid her forearm across her head. "Oh my GOD!"

"Are you okay?" Artie said after a moment.

She breathed in and out, deep, before finally exhaling. "No, Arthur, I'm not."

He shrugged and started to walk a bit closer.

"Don't." She didn't even look at him.

"Alright," he put his hands up and backed away back into the kitchen. He puffed a bit. "I mean, you know, I could've just let you catch a cold, didn't even have to bring you inside, but, yeah, that's fair."

"You're amazing," she sat up a bit and flashed a wide smile and batted her eyelashes. "Mr. Doon, you're the best."

"You're welcome," Artie mumbled. He leaned back on the sink and sighed before looking out the window again. He looked over to Holly—she was still sitting up on the couch. She looked awake, but under her eyes it was dark, and she sat with all the tension in her posture of someone who was used to having her seat pulled right out from under her.

Maybe what she needed now was space.

Artie headed upstairs and grabbed his fishing gear and his book. When he came down, Holly had laid back down. He poured himself a cup of coffee and turned around.

"I'm going fishing."

She looked at him, and her eyes narrowed, just a bit.

"You can come if you want."

She didn't say anything. He shrugged.

"If you're fine here, that's fine too. There's some coffee left," he gestured to the pot. "And we got plenty of movies if you get bored."

Holly didn't say anything. She looked away and closed her eyes.

Artie sighed and headed out the door.

He couldn't concentrate on his book. Artie closed the Western and stared out over the bay, the tip of his rod waving in the wind.

He'd been occupied over the past few months with how history would remember someone like him. Waterspell, at least his start there, had been four years ago, but it felt like decades—and in less than half a decade he'd been an accomplice to some of the greatest crimes against people, against kids, against the collective moral fiber of the human race, without even knowing it. Almost the literal definition of a stooge.

He could've asked more questions. He'd always felt like

something had been off at the school. But he'd just been happy to get a job with a film degree.

How guilty could he really be if he had been lied to every step of the way? He didn't know about what happened to each Senior class, the dosing, the isolation tanks, the surgeries. It wasn't like that was posted on the school criers—"By the by, this prep school is a front for human trials that'll make MKUltra look like Sunday school. And if you work here, and people find out, someday you'll be implicated as an asset to gross violations of human rights on a scale so mind-boggling the least you'll need to do is fake your own death to get peace of mind."

Artie sighed and scratched his cheek. He shouldn't have listened to Valentine. She'd been the prime reason he'd gotten so enamored with the whole project. She kept telling him about how the school was revolutionary, that the kids would go on to change the world.

Of course, at the time, he hadn't really understood what she meant, and it was only in hindsight that the double entendre behind her words made itself fully clear. He'd spent too much time and thought since then mulling over whether or not he was genuinely stupid, and had come to the conclusion that, at the time, he was more lightly apathetic and equipped with a one-track mind than anything. Getting the teaching position, having access to resources through the school for finishing his film, meeting Valentine.... he'd practically thought he'd died. And, in a way, when he took the job, he did.

There was a darker admission, though, which was that Artie had never felt more accepted than when he was at Waterspell. More a part of something. That was one of the most alluring parts of the school—there was this weird, palpable sense that something was wrong, and at the same time, that sense felt like some grand design. He found himself trying to decide, on more than one occasion, if it felt wrong because it actually was wrong, or if it felt wrong because it was something different. Something new. Something with a great potential for great change. Turns out, it had been both, to some degree.

Something tugged on the end of his rod. He jerked up once and the familiar weight settled on the end. He began to pull the line in.

-

When Artie got back, he found Holly asleep on the couch. She'd curled up in a ball, the blanket on the floor, barely taking up a cushion and a half. He went over and set the blanket back on her before going into the kitchen, grabbing his knives and cutting board, and heading back outside to clean the fish.

He sat in the lawn chair near the door and lit a Madoff, setting the cutting board on his lap and slapping the fish down on it.

Artie always felt a little bad, a little cold, filleting fish. At this point it'd become so routine that he could do it almost by sheer instinct and feeling alone, not even really needing to look at the fish while he cut in.

But it wasn't just instinct that kept him looking away— it was the eye. There was something in each eye of every fish he caught, one last wet bubble of life that stared back at him, preserved until he chucked them over the cliffs and back where they'd come from.  Sometimes, if he was really in a hurry, they'd still spasm a bit as he made the cuts along the head and down the spines.  It was a part of nature, he'd rationalized, and it didn't take much to rationalize it.  Things died in the most horrific natural ways all the time; many more lived in the most horrific natural ways, all the time.

He still found it a little sad though, to be confronted with the death of something, even a dumb fish, he'd personally set into motion that morning.  All because he wanted something to eat.

When he was finished, he went back inside, dug out the portable fryer from one of the lower cupboards under the counter, and started to lug it outside.  Holly mumbled something in her sleep and turned over.  He couldn't tell if she'd actually woken up and was pretending, or if she was genuinely still knocked out.  Maybe a bit of both.

In half an hour, the fish was fried up.

Artie set it and a few French fries on a paper plate and quietly went upstairs to change.  He threw on his suit, a shirt, slacks, and slipped on his shoes.  When he came down, Holly was still turned away.  No more mumbling.  Just faint, slow breathing.

He put the plate in the cooler and started off down the road.

The sad thing was, Waterspell had been the greatest single thing to happen in his life.  He'd never felt happier, or at the very least, like he had some small, bit—but still true and fulfilling—part to play in life. Before Waterspell, he'd been working as a clerk at a video store in the Minnesota northwoods.

He'd been chipping away at making his own film, an eighty-minute feature about a motorcycle gang up north, for almost two years. The crew was small and stripped-down—just him and a few of his friends. Everyone pulled double, triple, quadruple duty. It wasn't anything great, and Artie knew it wasn't going to be anything great. But it was a start.

Then Waterspell had called. A job, a real job, out East. Somewhere with production value. A position with actual income. Artie remembered how it just didn't feel real. He'd be able to strike out on his own, make some money, and finish the movie.

Well that hadn't happened.

As he turned off onto the path towards the shrine, he had to chuckle, just a bit. He'd barely been at Waterspell for four years before the entire world had almost literally collapsed on itself. And after that, he'd been labeled a monster adjacent, a blind criminal against humanity, and shunted away into a lighthouse on the far reaches of the cold Northeast.

He passed under the torii gate, did the sign of the cross, and made his way up and into the shrine. He knelt and closed his eyes, saying a silent prayer.

Then he got up and turned around.

Holly was standing about ten feet away from the bottom of the shrine's steps, watching him.

"What are you doing here?"

Artie shrugged. "Praying, I think. How'd you find me?"

"I saw you when you left. I wanted to see where you were going." She looked around. "It's pretty." Her eyes landed on him again, and they flashed for a moment with a younger, gotcha energy. "Isn't it illegal for you to be out here?"

Artie chuckled and sat on the steps. He took out a Madoff and lit. "You sound like your sister."

She sat down next to him. It was quiet. Nice, even.

Artie could tell, obviously, she was running from something. There was a clear and ringing paranoia, the tone of some far-off bell, the way she was constantly looking around, how she never seemed to relax. If he had to guess, it was Valentine. And that meant, sooner or later, she'd come here.

He groaned. Holly looked at him. "What?"

"Nothing," he waved his hand. "Just a bit of a headache."

"You shouldn't smoke those. That's probably what's doing it."

"Maybe, but I don't think so." He eyed her. "You want one?"

She thought for a moment and nodded. He handed her a Madoff, and the lighter, and she lit and inhaled. He knew the kids had used to smoke back in Waterspell. They'd sneak in cigarettes somehow, probably from one of the gas stations along the roads outlying the campus. He didn't blame them.

Artie turned to her after a while. "You wanna watch a movie tonight?"

She thought. And nodded.

\-

When they'd gotten back, after a fierce debate, they'd decided on watching *The Devil Wears Prada*. Artie hadn't necessarily been in favor, but Holly had countered that it was one of the only movies she could remember from his class, and remember liking, to boot. So they'd sat down and put it on.

He'd forgotten what it felt like to watch a movie with someone. It was almost as communal as sitting around a campfire, the way both people were tuned in to the exact same thing, but seemed lost in thought, drawn and kind of drowned in their own experience with the film. It produced an ambient warmth and calm that Artie had found comforting ever since he'd been a little boy. And it was always more than a little fun to talk about whatever you watched after it was all over.

About a third of the way through, he looked over at Holly. A thin film of sweat had broken out on her forehead. She winced once or twice at a shot change, like she'd been flicked in the temple.

"Hey, are you okay?" he leaned over.

"Mhmmm," she nodded. That was all he got. He couldn't help but feel concerned, but he didn't really know what to do. So they kept watching.

A few minutes later, Holly's breathing had become shallow, almost ragged. She kept clearing her throat, and her eyes would dart from the screen more and more. Artie didn't know if she was sick, or having a panic attack, or what. He paused the movie.

"Keep going."

"Holly—"

"Keep going!" Her voice rang loud, and clear, as though it'd been plugged in somewhere else. Artie pressed play.

A little over halfway through, Holly was soaked in sweat. She could barely keep her eyes on the screen. And her breath fluttered in and out of her chest.

Artie moved to pause—

"NO!"

He felt something, like a wave of air push him away.  Holly wasn't even looking at him anymore.  She was fixed on the television.

"Holly, you're not—"

"Stop!  STOP!"

She wasn't talking to him anymore.  He wasn't in the room.  She was shouting at the television, and her voice was rising to a fever pitch.  Tears rolled down her face.  Her voice was heavy, and choked.  "PLEASE!"

The T.V. screen began to crack.  Artie's eyes widened.

And then Holly screamed.

Artie was flung over the side of the couch and into the opposite wall, right into his *Jaws* poster.  The glass crunched and sprinkled down on him as he crumpled to the floor.  He barely managed to look up.

Between Holly and the television, the air looked waving, distorted, like the heated space above a campfire.  The glow of the television was amplified, almost ghostly, seeping out of the monitor in a fog and making its way over towards Holly.  She kept crying, sobbing, fat tears rolling down her face, shouting at the top of her lungs, "I LOVE YOU!  STOP!  PLEASE!  PLEASE!  DON'T YOU LOVE ME TOO?  DON'T YOU?!"

Another shockwave rippled out through the air, and Artie was knocked back into the wall, the back of his head wracking against the brick.  He saw stars and spots.  He had the sudden realization that whatever was going on could either kill him, or her, or the both of them, or it could draw attention.

So he stood up, a bit crouched, and made his way over to the couch.  It was like wading through a muddy lake bottom.

Just waves and waves of organic, thick energy, and they kept getting stronger.

He came behind Holly and looked up. The television was completely distorted, nothing but a swirling pool of milky white light, leaking out of the screen. If he concentrated, he thought he could see faces, faces that didn't belong in the movie. For a moment, he saw an older girl, olive skin, thin face, dark eyes, and a brilliant smile. And he got it. And his heart sank.

Artie put his hands on Holly's shoulders. A shiver wracked her body. He leaned down to her ear and, shouting over the din, said, "Holly! HOLLY! YOU'RE OKAY! YOU'RE HERE, HOLLY! IT'S JUST A MOVIE! YOU'RE SAFE!"

And for a moment, everything froze. All the sound was sucked out of the room in a single instant. The only thing moving or making noise was Holly, sniffing, sobbing.

And then, like a rubber band snapping, it released. And Artie was flung into the back wall, and saw nothing but black afterwards.

Chapter Three

The Last Day

Artie came-to on his couch, panting, gasping. He felt something cold and heavy slide off his head and slap onto the floor. He looked down—it was an icepack.

He looked around, wincing, splintering aches digging into his head.

Holly was in the kitchen, at the stove. Something was sizzling and popping. It smelled sweet, and crisp. Artie sighed. That was probably the bacon he'd gotten. He'd been saving it for a special occasion, or whenever his will broke and he made it. But he supposed now was as good a time as any.

She turned around. It looked like she hadn't slept at all. "Hey."

Artie managed a smile and felt more pains crack through his skull. "Hi." He groaned and laid back down.

A few minutes later, he heard Holly come over and set something down on the coffee table. He opened his eyes and looked over. It was a fork, a knife, and a plate of really, really well-done sunny-side eggs, and charred bacon. And a cup of coffee that looked so black it may as well have been a hole in reality.

"Looks good," he said after a moment. He sat up, careful, as his back and his forehead stitched. She sat down in the armchair and watched him, legs crossed, hands folded.

He cut into the eggs, which crackled like potato chips, and speared a piece of one of the bacon strips, most of which crumbled into black powder the moment he tried. He scooped the chunks onto his fork with his knife and brought them into his mouth. It tasted like fried gasoline.

Artie looked up at Holly. He nodded and smiled, and swallowed. "Wow. It's, uh," he coughed and thumped his chest, instinctively taking a sip of coffee. It felt like grainy black pudding going down. For a breath, his voice left his body, and he replied in a faint wheeze. "It's all very... present." He coughed again.

She tried to smile, but it left her face before she could keep it. "I'm sorry."

"What?" he shook his head. "No, this is great."

"About what happened."

"Ah," Artie said, mouth half-opened, and he nodded. His eyes were on his plate. "Yeah. I mean, I know it's not Oscar material, but I don't think the movie's, you know, *that* bad."

"Artie."

He looked up and felt guilt settle in his stomach along with the charred bacon and eggs. For the first time since he'd met Holly years ago, the shine of a challenge in her eyes was dim. Almost non-existent. Her face really did look so much older.

"I used to watch that movie a lot with my sister when we were growing up," she said after a little while. "I know it's kinda dumb, but being so far apart, I felt so grown-up and included when we watched it, you know?  It was like, 'Wow, my sister, my *sister*, wants to show me a grown-up movie. She thinks I'm cool enough.'"  Holly laughed, soft.  "And so, of course it'd be my favorite when you showed it in class, you know."

Holly looked Artie in the eyes.  "Do you know what they used your movies for?  Why they had you show them to us?"

Artie shook his head.  Holly took a deep breath, and exhaled, slow.

"They were for Room 3A."

Artie's heart pounded, and he reeled, momentarily lost.

Room 3A had been Waterspell's psychoactive battery facility, a special unit designed to break a subject's psychological frame beyond recognition.  Each student was mass-dosed with a psychoactive cocktail, then isolated in Room 3A, strapped down, and made to watch whatever the administrators threw up on the screen, during which they were also subjected to occasional "stress assessments", which usually involved electro-shocks, oxygen deprivation, and "moderate physical trauma." Sometimes sessions could last for over thirty-six straight hours.  And that was only what was released about 3A in the official public reports—there was certainly more that had been done that the public would never, and they were lucky, hear about.

Artie hadn't known about 3A until after the October Sentence.  Every facility like Waterspell, and there had been dozens across the country, used their own version of 3A.  It was the final gauntlet the program had used before deciding which candidates were ready to be offered a position.  Of course, all those who'd graduated had been scooped up by the Interior, and reassigned as permanent assets to stations all over the world. Which brought up that screaming, distant thought in the back of Artie's head with a final confirmation that someone, somewhere, was coming for Holly.

He leaned forward and put his head in his hands. Holly watched him. "Fuck me. And I helped them do it. For four years."

There were a lot of ideas about what to do with someone who was willingly, knowingly, and above all, actively complicit and driving behind wrongs and evils. String them up, punish them, send them to the furthest corners of the Earth. Banish them from all realms of thought and idea. Keep them forever in the minds of whoever knew about them as an agent of evil, a transgressor against the light of the human soul.

But what about people who were the nuts and bolts of the systems of evil? What about the accountants, the janitors, the day in, day out employees in an office where they were treated with, at best, passive ignorance, an elite disdain for the unimportant, unenlightened members of the workforce that propped up an entire network of abused power. Without them, the office didn't run. The engine didn't turn. Nothing could happen if the nuts and bolts weren't in place. Did that make them as culpable? If anything, maybe it made them moreso, even if they were completely and totally, or at least relatively, unaware. What was their punishment? What were their sins? And, if they wanted to, how could they atone for crimes that they laid the track for?

Artie looked up at Holly and her distant eyes. His own drifted to the television.

He looked back over to her after a moment.

"Wanna help me make a movie?"

He set up the tripod where it had been a couple days ago when he'd been getting the final shot.  The sky was cold and grey, though a bit of sun in long waving beams shown in the distance down on Wharfton, an old collection of scrunched-together homes and small businesses and a couple churches and docks clustered on the edge of the cliffs.  A fishing village from an age or so past.

Holly stood a few feet away as he futzed with the legs, tightening them.  The camera case was at his feet.  She made a move forward.

"Don't."

"I can help."

"Let me get it set up first."

She took the same step back.  She was impatient.  He'd worked with worse.

"Have you ever been over there?"

Artie knelt down and unlatched his camera case.  Inside was an olive green film camera that looked like it'd been hammered out of raw scrap from a decommissioned Normandy landing craft.  A trio of swiveling lenses of different lengths, fat metal eyes the thickness of miniature soup cans, sat idle on the face.  He hefted the camera up with the tender, if somewhat tired, care a pet owner would give to a drowsy old animal, and carefully brought it onto the tripod mount.  Artie clicked it into place.

"Alright."

"Did you hear what I said?" she was looking at him, a hard, bored expression on her face.

He sighed and scratched at the bottom of his chin with the tip of his thumb.  He looked past her at the town and thought before going back to her.  "I'm not allowed.  Remember?"

Before she could answer, he gestured her over.  Curt irritation crossed her face, but it evaporated quick in the light of curiosity.

"Okay," he started as she came over to check out the camera.  "'I've got one roll of film left."  He pointed to a counter on the side of the camera.  A thin black ticker hovered a little under the number **100**.  "See that?  That's a hundred feet."

"Is that a lot?"

"It's about two minutes, give or take."

"That's not a lot."

"No it's not.  So," he pointed down the road where the camera was angled.  "You can't press down on this," he thumbed a small button on the back of the camera, "until about five or so seconds until I come down that road.  You'll hear me."

"What're you coming down on?"

"My motorcycle."

She laughed.  "You have a motorcycle?"

"What?"

"Nothing," she waved, still laughing a bit.  "Cool, man."

"This is the only shot I have left.  After that I'm done."

"What's happening?"

"I... uh," Artie rubbed the back of his head.  He found himself getting... flustered wasn't the right word.  She was a kid, he didn't have anything to prove to her.  It was more, he realized, the fact that he hadn't talked with someone about what he was making in a long time.

He cleared his throat. "I was... am... making a movie about a motorcycle gang in the northwoods. And this is the last shot where my guy gets to the meeting spot they all decided on, and no one's there."

"And then it ends?"

"And then it ends."

"That's sad."

He shrugged. "That's what it is." He looked around. The light was still holding. He'd shot enough to know the rough focus and exposure for the times of day around the lighthouse, but he didn't want to chance anything. "Okay. So you think you know what to do?"

She nodded.

"Cool," he started back towards the lighthouse garage. "Remember, wait 'till I come around."

An hour later, they'd done a couple takes. It took Artie about five minutes to drive down and back, and another fifteen was sandwiched in there as he talked with Holly about the shot.

Eventually, the light had changed to the point where it would be noticeable even on the black and white film stock, and Artie decided to call it a day. He and Holly packed up the equipment and lugged it inside. He asked her if she'd want to go fishing with him, and after a pause, she said yes.

They both headed down to his rock, him carrying the

fishing pole and the cooler, her the tacklebox and his two lawn chairs.

He set the pole against the rock as she opened the folding chairs.  She sat down, so did he, and they were there for a few minutes in the quiet after he cast out.

"You can actually catch fish?"

He looked over at her.  She looked at him.

"Yeah," he went back to looking out over the Atlantic.

"How?"

"I don't know," he said after a hesitation.  He shrugged.  "It just happens."

"Every day?"

"Most days."

"Do you like it?"

"It passes the time."

"Do you like it here?"

He sighed and bent down, reached into the cooler, and grabbed a beer.  He offered her one and she took it, snapping the tab and taking a drink.

Artie had to smile a bit, to himself, just in the appreciation of company.  He sipped from the can.  The foam tasted like fizzing bread.

"So?"

"Listen, Holly, I don't wanna... like... get into it here, you know.  You don't wanna know that stuff.  Don't you hate me?"

"I don't hate you," she said.  She sniffed and rubbed her nose.  "I just didn't like you when you dated Valentine."

"Jealous?"

"Gross."

He thought for a half a minute, took a couple more sips, and sighed again. "I think the thing that sucks the most is how pretty it is here."

She looked over at him. No interruption. He continued.

"I can hear them sometimes, over in that town," he nodded his head with an absent note in the direction of Wharfton. "They must've had some kind of Christmas Parade or market or something. I heard bells and carols for a week straight. After that, fireworks on New Year's. After that, fights and really bad plastic paddy music on St. Paddy's Day. After that, fireworks again for the Fourth. But through all of it, I hear the quiet the most." He sipped again. "You know. The wind coming off the coast and mixing with the waves. The birds. I get to feel the sun, and I get to see the clouds, and I wonder what it would all look like, feel like, sound like, be like, if I lived in that little town." He drained his can and crumpled it, a reflex. He set down the can carefully and scooped another from the cooler. "But I'll never know." He cracked the tab and drank. "So I don't like to think about it a lot."

They sat there in the quiet again.

Holly cleared her throat.

"I thought of another end for your movie."

Chapter Four

Film-O

"I'm hungry."

Artie started with a snort. He sat up, slow, rubbing his eyes. There was a cracking pain in the back of his neck. He rubbed it with a sluggish hand.

He'd fallen asleep, he realized, at his editing desk again. It wasn't so much a desk as a small pop-up end table he'd stuffed in the closet in his room. On top was a miniature station for cutting up the film he developed with a cruddy mail-order at-home development tank, darkroom bag, and chemicals he kept stored in his bottom dresser drawer. Torn tongues of tape licked out from the edge of the table. Scraps of film littered the floor and tabletop, little celluloid snowflakes from countless late-night flurries. The film hung in strips, like laundry on a clothesline, between the two spools. A Film-O visor, a small glass and metal monitor that acted as a magnifying glass for each frame that passed underneath it, showed a frame from the new ending. A small figure, Holly in frozen miniature, stood there, waiting in front of the lighthouse. She thought it would be a bit better—have his character find someone at the very end. He didn't know how he felt about it, but he had a feeling it was probably gonna stay in.

Scattered around the station were beer cans, crushed, and a couple bottles, some opaque from age, others too clear and empty to be anything other than shameful.  Artie rubbed his eyes again and turned around.

Holly was behind him, arms folded.

He blinked.  "I can make eggs or something."

She made a noise in the back of her throat.  "I'm sick of eggs and fish."

"So am I," he stood up and stretched.  Several disturbing but relieving snaps greeted his lower back as he did.  He winced and sighed and walked past Holly.

"We should go somewhere," she said, following as he walked down the stairs.  "I bet they've got great food in that town."

He looked back at her, a half-frown, half-smile on his face.  A kind of knowing settled in his gut.  "We can't do that."

"Please."

Artie waved his hand as he made his way into the kitchen.  He clicked on the front right burner for the stove and went to the fridge, grabbing the egg carton.

"You want sunny-side or scrambled?  I think..." he bent down, peering further into the fridge.  "Yeah, we've still got some cheese and bacon.  You want some of that?"

Holly pulled up one of the stools on the counter and sat down.  She leaned forward, her chin resting on her arms.  Her eyes were a bit resigned, a bit disappointed, and still more than a bit dogged.  "I really don't want any eggs."

"Toast?  Bacon?"

"Arthur."

He set the carton down on the slim stretch of counter by

the stove, squatted down, took out a pan from the bottom oven drawer, and set it on the burner.

"It'd be really fun."

Artie took out an egg and made to crack it... but hesitated. He sighed and turned around.  "We can't."

"We could."

"Why do you want to go so bad?"

She thought for a moment.  "I've never had a good cup of coffee."

The statement hung in the air.

"Never?"

"Nuh uh."

Artie looked at her, then back to the pan, the burner, and the egg in his hand.

He turned the burner off and flipped up the carton lid, nestling the egg back in its stiff cardboard bed.  He turned around.

"Alright."

He waited for her out by the garage, leaning on his bike. The morning was bright and cool, the sky a wide new blue mingling with the warming light from the sun as it just started its day.  A thin frosting of clouds clung to the horizon, some kind of great mist emerging from the Atlantic as the ocean met the sky.

Holly came out the front door with the camera case in her hand.

"What are you doing?"

She shrugged and lifted the case a little. "I figured we could use the last of the film and get something from today."

He was frustrated for a moment... but it passed with his breath in the cold air. Going into town was already putting himself and her right on the chopping block. She was right. May as well get something if they could. May as well make something.

He climbed on the bike and she got on the back, wrapping her arms under his armpits.

"I'm not gonna fall off, am I?"

"If you do, try and save the camera."

She laughed as he kicked off and they sped down the road.

-

They followed the road along the Atlantic, a lean country strip that didn't have a name, and reached the outskirts of Wharfton in less than half an hour, which weren't much more than a few warehouses and distant East Coast homesteads settled on a gentle incline. Below the hill, the warehouses became less skeletal, fuller, newer, and the houses grew closer and closer together until they were practically on top of each other in an urban latticework of homes and small factories and shops. Cars trundled like little glinting beetles through the network of cramped streets.

The motorcycle made its way down the hill and further into the city. There was an empty parking lot behind a brown two-story brick drug store, and Artie pulled off into the back area and set the bike up.

"Okay," he clapped his hands together. "We probably shouldn't be here too long, so what do you wanna do?"

Holly thought for a moment. "Coffee?"

Artie nodded. "Coffee."

They headed out from the parking lot and down the street. It was still quiet, even in what was slowly becoming mid-morning, but there were a few people out and about. A city truck rumbled past them, a couple street workers in neon orange sweatshirts bobbing up and down on the back flatbed. One waved to the two of them. Holly waved back.

It had been almost a year, Artie realized, since he'd taken a walk outside around other people. He felt naked. There was a yawning terror... but it was countered by a greater, unfolding hunch of a sort of freedom.

Parked on the side of the road was a dented, squashed-looking silver food truck, a rejected space-age caravan type that looked like it'd crashed into the moon and fallen back down to Earth. There was a swirled robin's-egg-blue label on the side: MAC'S KITCHEN. The "K" was punched-in, no doubt a battlescar from its cross-stellar fight to get back planetside. Holly stopped and jerked her head at it.

Artie looked it up and down. "I don't know if they sell coffee."

She was already up at the open window. A fat, rumpled, tan man with pockmarked cheeks and a smudged apron came to the window. "What can I getcha hon."

"Coffee, please."

"Anything else?"

She looked back at Artie. He came up to the window. She turned around. "Two coffees."

"What size?"

"Medium," said Artie.

"Medium," said Holly.

"Anything in 'em?"

"Black," said Artie.

"Black," said Holly.

The guy nodded and headed into the dim guts of the truck. Something sizzled in the back. The scent of crisped meat and salt-and-pepper eggs trickled slowly through the open window.

Holly nudged Artie's side. He looked down at her, and she raised her eyebrows a couple times. He shrugged and she laughed.

The guy came back with two stubby foam cups capped with flimsy plastic lids.

"Five eighty-five."

Artie dug in his coat pocket for his wallet and rifled out a clump of crumpled dollar bills. He laid them out on the counter. There were seven.

"Out of seven."

"You can just keep the change."

The guy nodded and waved the wrinkled fan of cash. He cocked his head as Artie took his cup. Soft heat leaked through the foam. "I don't think I've ever seen you two around here before."

Artie nodded and, for a moment, a sting of panic twanged his chest. "We just moved to the area."

The guy pursed his lips, the bottom sticking out in a kind of fat approval. "Well. Welcome to Wharfton, bud." He turned to Holly and nodded again. "Lady."

Holly flourished with her free hand. They thanked the food truck guy and headed down the street.

Holly took a few tentative sips from her cup. She smacked her lips.

"It's hot."

"That's how you know it's good."

"It kinda sucks."

"That's also how you know it's good."

She kept sipping every so often.

They wandered to an intersection. To the right, what must have been a part of the downtown, or maybe the whole downtown, Artie had no idea, stretched on in a quiet up-and-down grace. Short brick buildings, department stores, barber shops, bars, and a coffee house or two, were all grouped together, huddled around the little cobblestone river where the occasional car passed by with the lethargy of a big aquarium fish. To the left, the road dipped down a hill, whatever buildings in the middle were obscured. But beyond, at the bottom, the road opened to a grid of old docks who commiserated with each other like drinking buddies, old friends.

He heard a whirring and jumped for a moment, turning at the same time. Holly had pointed the camera at him, most of her face obscured, except for the sliver of a toothy gotcha grin that peeked out behind the eyepiece.

Artie stood there for a moment, watching her, before looking straight into the lens. He leaned forward and she laughed, trying to back up. "It's gonna mess up the focus."

"Ah," he waved his hand, standing up again and taking a sip from his coffee. It had already begun to cool down.

Grounds swam in his mouth like grains of sand.  Roughage, that what his Dad had used to say.  "It'll look like a Beastie Boys video."

"So, corny?" Holly said as she lowered the camera.

"Some of the best things are."

He looked around the intersection.  "Alright.  You pick.  Which way?"

Holly looked right, then left, and hung on the left for a moment.  "I wanna see those."  She pointed at the docks and looked back at him.  "Do you think we can get on one?"

"Let's see."

They headed to the left.  The middle part of the hill, the obscure chunk, the unknown land, rolled out into a few small apartments and dilapidated, or at least urbanely rustic, homes.  A couple people dotted the porches, mainly older and greyer.  Some of them had coffees.  Others smoked.  One was reading a book.  They all, at one point, watched the two kids walking down the hill, for just a couple moments or so, before going back to the theater of the morning as the curtains rose.

"Is this anywhere like where you grew up?"

Holly looked at him.  She sipped her coffee.

He thought.  His mouth worked, and he sighed, a profuse exhale from his nose.  "Not really, no."

"What do you mean?"

"Well, we never had a view like this where I come from," he gestured with his coffee hand to Wharfton's bay.  The sky was a crude orange, dulling above to a faint and far away yellow, ending in a new blue.  "It's mostly just fields and trees.  When it snows, it's really nice.  But the rest of the year... I don't know.  It's home.  I can't hate it, not really.  But this is…" he looked around.  "This is different."  He looked over at her.  "What about you, Kubrick?"

"What, Valentine didn't tell you where she was from?"

"Montana, right?"

"Colorado."

"Oh.  Well… yeah, she did.  But I wanna hear what you thought about it."

She looked over the bay as she walked.  Her steps were full of a kind of loose purpose, a fading teenage confidence carrying her feet.  "It was pretty."

"You sound disappointed."

"I was.  It sucks when something pretty hurts you.  It makes you feel lost."

They reached the docks after another ten minutes or so of walking.  Both of them followed along one of the breakwaters, to the crook in its elbow.  They sat down on the edge, feet dangling a ways over the waves splashing up against the wall, throwing up cold spray.  Somewhere, in the town that now felt distant behind them, a train whistled through the buildings and streets.

They both sat there a while, and then something occurred to Artie, and he motioned to the camera case.  Holly looked him over before before handing it to him.  He took out the Bolex and fiddled with the focus and exposure.  It might have been a little over or under, but maybe that would make it more genuine.

He started filming.  She stared right at him, past the lens.

"Wanna hear a joke?"

"Sure," she said.

He told it to her, an old one about a farmer with a three-legged pig. There wasn't any sound recording on the Bolex—no one watching the film would ever hear the joke. She was the only one. And at the end, as he finished, she laughed. It was a lame, dumb, old joke. But she laughed, against the splashing sea and the gray sky. In the frame, just a sliver of Wharfton, bits and pieces of the docks, and a slim arm of houses clinging to the bay, were visible. A quiet background to a silent joke.

Artie put the camera away afterwards and gave it back to her.

They stayed in Wharfton until the late evening, walking around, talking, filming, grabbing food from food trucks that hung around cramped streets like stray dogs. By the time they left, the city lights were beginning to wink on, one by one. They rode out from where they'd come in under warm orange blurring streetlamps, the lights from house windows and warehouses waving a sort of goodbye as they passed, memorial candles. It was like a distant picture, even when they were in it, one they'd only seen from miles away. And for once, they got to know what it felt like, up close.

## Chapter Five

Sisters

Artie woke up, face-down, resting on his arms, in his editing closet.

He sat up slow, rubbing his eyes, and stretching into a yawn.

And then he heard something.  A rumbling.

There was a hurried scuffling up the stairs.  Holly burst into his room.  Her face was pale.  Before Artie could ask, a voice, amplified and somewhat distorted and crackling from a loudspeaker, spoke outside.

"Holly Navarro!  It's your sister!  I'm here to take you home!"

A little, happy laugh came at the end of the sentence, like the voice had been party to some game known to but a few, and the owner had just won the whole pot.  The loudspeaker clipped off in the middle of the laugh.

"Oh, great," Artie groaned, with more nonchalance than he felt.  His legs and arms shook a bit as he stood up.  He had a headache, and realized, with a foggy and slightly disappointed lurch, that he'd been drinking last night.  The clusters of bottles all around his desk had swelled their ranks.

Holly was still in the doorway.  He looked at her.

"Stay inside," he said, pushing past her.

Holly grabbed his arm.  He didn't turn around.  "She'll kill you."

He shrugged, partially to try and put on his best slouching, who-cares, slacker cowboy air he'd learned from older guys and movies, to try and calm her down, and partially to shake her off.  "She hasn't seen me in a year.  Maybe she'll be happy."

Artie went down the hall, descended the stairs, and crossed the living room.  He stopped at the door, paused for a moment with his hand wrapped around the handle.  It was cool.

He opened the door.

About twenty feet down the road was a white '69 Volkswagen Bus with evergreen detailing, parked at an angle along the road.  A couple people stood just a few feet beyond it. One looked like a really tall girl, with long, straight hair, wearing a navy draped trench coat, some sleeveless cream top underneath, brown slacks, and boots.  She had a wide-brimmed black hat with a sort of floppy, pointed top.  Next to her was a shorter East-Asian guy, in black sunglasses and a full suit.  Artie squinted.  They gave off the impression of new professionals.  Even with all their posturing, there was something ironically amateur about them.  Like they were kids in some school play.

On top of the van, holding a microphone snaking its way back into the cab, was another figure.  A woman with dark

Bacall hair in a baggy black long sleeve turtleneck sweater, with loose houndstooth trousers and black boots. She had a casual, lithe grace to her, and was pacing with wide, almost comical steps across the top of the van. When she turned back towards the lighthouse, he knew she saw him.

"Oh my God," she said, into the loudspeaker.

She hopped down in a smooth arc from the van, like she weighed nothing, and walked towards him.

"So this is where she ran off to," Valentine said, with the full, crinkling smile of an unexpected reunion. "She's been staying with you."

Before Artie could say anything, she threw her arms around his neck and pulled him in close. Her cheek rested in the groove between his neck and shoulder. There was a scent around her, something faint and absently pretty. She whispered, "I missed you."

It had been over a year since Artie had hugged anyone. He leaned into her.

"So," Valentine said, pulling away, her arms still hooked around his neck, her eyes looking right into his. "She's inside?"

"Yeah," Artie tried to turn to show her, but she kept him locked in place.

"Has she been okay?"

"She's scared."

She put her bottom lip out. "I know. The past few months have been really tough. She barely passed her Finals, you know. Doesn't have that push I had. But she did it."

Artie nodded. He couldn't help but notice her eyes

darting for a moment around him. Always looking. Always working.

"Why'd she run away?"

"Oh, you know. She's afraid she won't do well wherever the Interior puts her. I've been trying to tell her, though, you know, that kind of attitude's a waste of time. If she wasn't something special she wouldn't be where she was. But she wouldn't listen, and the next thing you know, I woke up and got a call that she didn't show up to her assignment posting." Val rolled her eyes. She may as well have been talking about a kid who'd played hooky from grade school, some innocent action in an innocent place. "So, naturally, I had to come looking for her. I was so worried, you know, but now..." her hands started to move.

He grabbed them, and Artie saw a stab of immediate irritation under a thin smile. He lowered them, carefully.

"I'm happy to see you too," he said, and the full smile returned.

She brought one of her hands up to his cheek. "You didn't deserve what they did. I wanted to keep you from the worst of what was coming."

Her voice was full of a twilight honesty. He wanted to believe her more than anything.

"I'll go in and talk with her," he said finally.

"Five minutes," Valentine said with a smile.

Artie closed the door and sank against it. The floor was

cold and a bit wet on the seat of his pants.  He put his fore-head on his crossed arms and sighed through the gap.

"I'm not going with her."

He looked up.  Holly was peeking around the stairs.  She slowly came down and said again, "I mean it.  I'm not going with her.  She's crazy, you know that."

"She's not crazy.  No one's crazy," Artie said, lifting his head up a bit and rubbing his cheeks.

"You're kidding, right?" Holly punctuated this with a short, barking laugh.

"She won." Artie looked up.  Holly was at the bottom of the stairs.  She looked so much like a little kid, like she was five or six and had just been informed by a weary parent that cartoons were fake and most everything she enjoyed wasn't at all, in one sense or another, real.

Artie got up and went to the kitchen.  He looked out the window for a moment before turning around and lighting a Madoff.  He leaned on the counter, quiet.

"She won," he said after a while.  "She did.  And she knows it.  I'm the one in custody here, indefinitely.  Not her.  She can do whatever she wants.  And most everyone will believe her.  Because she won."

"Stop saying that."

"Look around Holly!" he swept his arm in a half-hearted arc at the shattered poster, the cigarette cartons, the broken television, the couch, the chair, the rug, all of it.  "All this is mine.  But none of it belongs," he jabbed a finger at the door.  "Out there anymore.  Most of the people out there think that people like me made all this shit," he swept his arm around again, a bit more frantic, a bit more ragged, a bit more sad, "to trick them.  I saw the newscasts.  I watched them burn old movies.  They hate anything to do with the world I wanted to be a part of.  I was barely starting, and before I knew it, I lost.  I fucking lost."

He went to the couch and sat down.  Artie stared at the wall and raised the cigarette to his mouth.  "I'm no one," he inhaled and exhaled, smoke pouring out of his face in place of tears.  He should have been able to cry.  He didn't know why he couldn't.

He sat there, with his head against the wall and the cigarette hanging limp in his mouth, smoke curling into his eyes.  He sniffed.  Holly watched him for a moment.

She came around and sat down next to him.  She leaned her head against his shoulder.  He didn't think much of it.  They could've fallen asleep for the rest of the afternoon for all he cared.

"I'll go after you finish the movie."

He looked over.  She looked up at him and nodded.

"She's not gonna like that."

"I don't care," she said, leaning her head back against his shoulder and closing her eyes.  "I really don't care."

–

Five minutes later, Artie walked out from the lighthouse, gently closed the door behind him, and headed over to Valentine.  She was talking hushed, but excitedly, with the tall girl.  As he lit a Madoff, she turned around at the sound of the flicks—he was surprised how she heard them, he was a good twenty feet away.

As he approached, she did too, and they met halfway.

"That was a little longer than five minutes," she said.

"She's stubborn," he took a drag and looked around. "Hey those hats aren't, like, official, right? Because that would be really embarrassing, Val."

"Arthur," Valentine came up close, smiling. "I know you're upset. I promise I'll come back after this is all over, I will. But right now, I would really, really love to get my sister back to where she's supposed to be. She's my responsibility."

"She was," Artie nodded. He frowned. "And you lost it."

She blinked. "Excuse me?"

"She'll be here one more night," Artie said. He exhaled. "She has to get her stuff packed. And then she'll come out."

"Right," Valentine folded her arms. She laughed. "Mhmm... Artie," she leaned in close. "I know a secret."

"What's that?"

"I saw you leave."

He pulled back—her hands grabbed his jacket and yanked him close again.

"You didn't think I wouldn't know? You didn't think I'd ever find out?" she pouted and pushed him back. He stumbled a bit, caught his foot on a rock, and fell flat on his ass. She squatted down over him, a cool ocean wind tugging at her hair, clouds drifting overhead.

"You've got until tomorrow morning," she said. "After that, I'm coming in."

She stood up and walked back to the van. She never looked back.

It wasn't until later that night that Artie finished the final edit. He sat there for a while, watching the film thread together.

He dug out his old projector from deep in the closet. And he watched it.

A little over an hour later, it was over. He flipped off the projector and sighed. That was it. Six years of work. And it was an amateur move. His one shot was a cruddy student film that he was embarrassed to say was his.

He went downstairs.

Holly was on the sofa. Paul Newman, through the cracked glass, was splayed out across the screen, shirt off, gut distended.

Artie went to the fridge and reached for the beer. But his hand stopped short, and he quietly shut the fridge and went instead to the freezer. Inside was a chilled bottle of cheap whiskey. He didn't bother getting a glass. He walked to the couch and sat down, unscrewed the cap, stared at the eye of the opening for a few moments before tipping it back. He gagged a bit and let himself sink back into the couch.

Holly looked over at him.

"How was the movie?"

Artie didn't say anything.

"Can I have some?"

He handed Holly the bottle.

She drank from it for a few seconds and gasped afterwards. "That tastes like root beer and nail polish." She took another drink.

"So you didn't like it?" Holly stretched her arm out and

handed the bottle back to him. Artie took it, tapped the neck for a minute, thinking. He took a drink. "I don't know. It's not that it's bad. It's just not good. It's kind of embarrassing, actually."

"Even the parts with us?"

"Those are okay. But they don't fit," he drank again and rubbed his face. "It's a mess. I should just scrap it."

"Can we watch it?"

He looked over at her. She looked over at him. Her eyes flickered with the screen. She looked a bit sleepy and far away.

"You don't want to."

"I do."

"That's how you wanna spend your last night here?"

"Yeah." She nodded. Something crossed her face for a moment. Her expression faltered. "I don't want it to be my last night here, Arthur."

She turned to the T.V.. Artie saw her features working, under the skin, to keep it together. Nothing noticeable unless you knew what to look for. A little twitch of the nose. Brushing hair back over her ear, and her fingers shook. Her small, pointed jaw working every once in a while. Artie could almost feel that wet, heavy sensation that coated the tongue and fogged up into the nose, what came before tears. He had no idea what he could do for her.

"Alright," he said, standing up, a bit shaky. He steadied himself and made his way around the couch. "We'll watch the movie."

He wished he had something better to give her. But he hoped, at the very least, a crappy little movie she'd helped make would be, in some ways, enough.

Chapter Six

The Last Picture Show

Artie woke up that morning and went downstairs. He looked around the living room—the couch was ruffled up, its blanket in a heap. But no sign of Holly.

His heart started to pound.

"Holly?"

He ran outside. Sparse grey clouds swam in the sky, a cold oil painting. The van Valentine and the other two had come in was gone.

And that's when he realized, just like that, she'd gone. She'd left.

He made to head back inside, but when he reached the door, he just turned around. One of the lawn chairs was leaned up against the side of the house. He unfolded it and sat down.

Artie was there for a while. He dug out his Madoffs and lit one.

It was funny how some of the most significant moments in your life always seemed to happen while you were away. Really the only stake you had in them was what you did after they took place. He wondered if that was the regular pattern, or if it was just through his own lacking that he'd never really been present for the deciding points in his life. Artie didn't really have any idea what the answer was. And he felt like even if he knew, it wouldn't bring much peace. It might not even help at all. Things would carry on like they always had, and knowing how they did, or why, wouldn't change the outcome.

He wiped his mouth and smoke crinkled into his eye. It watered and he rubbed it and sniffed. Just like that, he was alone again.

He snubbed out the cigarette and stood up.

And something occurred to him then. He'd wanted to say goodbye. He'd really wanted to say goodbye.

He went back inside and found the film.

And he went out to the garage. Opened the door. He looked at the old chopper for a moment and climbed on.

There was a point in everyone's life where they had to make that decision. The one the movies and books and songs and paintings and shows and all the stories talked about, even if they didn't know it. It could take years, or it could happen in a moment. It was the point where a person was either in the audience of their own life again, or, for a single moment, walked onto the screen and made their own direction. However long that moment on the screen, that moment of action, lasted, wasn't really up to them. At any time, fate could close the curtains or snap the film or shout "Fire!" or knock over the projector altogether. What mattered, what really mattered, was what they did with the time they were given.

Artie kicked the throttle and roared out down the road.

He caught up to them a quarter mile from Salsbury Point. The van was steaming along, a white pillbox bullet, by the arcing coast and gray ocean.

Without hesitation, he came right up alongside. Holly was in the passenger's seat. Her eyes widened when she saw him. Valentine looked over and her face drew pale. In a moment, Holly opened the door, jumped on the back of the motorcycle, and Artie shoved the throttle forward as hard as he could. They tore off, leaving the van and Valentine and the rest behind.

They got to Wharfton in record time. As Artie wound the cycle through the close-knit roads and hilly side streets towards the train station, he still had a feeling Valentine wasn't far off. That was alright. He could always worry later.

They pulled into the station and hopped off the bike, both of them running at full tilt, over the gates, past the guards and ticket takers, and onto the platform.

Artie hugged her goodbye and handed her the film. She looked at him, the reel in her hands, and threw her arms around her and hugged him again. He hugged her back.

"Thank you."

He didn't say anything. He just squeezed a little harder.

She broke away and ran onto the train.

Artie watched it pull out. By the time Valentine arrived, he wasn't doing anything other than sitting on a bench and looking at the clouds ahead.  There was a little patch of blue sky just beginning to break through the gray.  For the first time, he felt like he'd done something.  He felt alone.  And he was okay.

# Concept Art

**Early Stage "Duds" Concept Art**
*Jayne Costello*

**Early Stage "St. Paddy's Day, 2032" Concept Art**
*Jayne Costello*

**Big Jay's Gas and Grill Concept Art**
*Jayne Costello*

**Early Stage "The Midnight God" Concept Art**
*Jayne Costello*

**Early Stage "CradL" Concept Art**
*Jayne Costello*

Japanese mask No face ┌ wood grain
• <u>midnight god</u> : [ Wong-She-tong
  swamp thing, owl face, texture
  of fur, fuffy fur, faded
  out, horns/ears, eery,

• <u>marlian apple</u>: Brighter colors,
  violets, blues, + yellows,

<u>font</u> :   ┌ colors (Novella)
— october, windy/breezy, wisconsin
  weather,
⋆ lighthouse space = big, connection
  between two characters

– Color pallet from photographs
  ⟶ lighthouse concepts

"BRIGHT"!
⟶ Slaughter
  house five
  inspiration

• <u>Back</u>: midnight god ⟶ see James
  sketch, narrow & tight, exchaning
  a hand, panel in a comic
  ⟶

• Icons : animal crossing style,
  Reference photos of face,

◦ Harris = older w/glasses

**Concept Art Notes**
*Jayne Costello*

**Concept Art for "The Phantom of the Pass" (Cut Story)**
*Jayne Costello*

**Concept Art For "Neon Clockwork Love" (Cut Story)**
*Jayne Costello*

AIR MAIL

THE POSTCARD STORIES

James Kuckkan
+
Jayne Costello

**End Title Card**
*Jayne Costello*

# Acknowledgements

My first thanks goes out to the group of family, friends, and readers who took the time over two years to read what I sent them and offered honest feedback and support.  Thank you Mom, Dad, Elizabeth, Mike, Grandma Kileen, Zander, Missy, Maddie, R.J., John, Calvin, Matt, Silas, Grant, Kyle, Meredith, Patrick, Barrett, Donald, and Holly.  Without your contributions, any of them, no matter what they were, this book wouldn't be.

I'd also like to thank Jayne, not just for her art, but for her time and patience.  She helped me out with this book during a time in her life where she was already being asked to do so much, and then she had to deal with someone who never really figured out video conferencing software.  She has been a constant inspiration since I've known her, and she and her art deserve the world.

I've lived in a few places over the past several years, and I'd like to send a thanks to Watertown, Milwaukee, Whitewater, Marquette, and Iowa City for not just providing me with different shades of experience that colored this book, but also good friends who have all made what can only be called a truly genuine impact on my life.

I'd like to send a special thanks to the Parchment Lounge and all its members. You were the first group I ever read a full piece of writing from the book to, and your encouragement and reception is something I'll treasure for a long, long time to come. I am incredibly fortunate to have met such a singularly great group of writers and people.

Finally, I'd like to thank the Watertown Street Department. I told them I was going to write a book a couple years ago, and I finally did, so I figured now would be as good a time as any to let them know I didn't forget. I don't know if this is the type of thing they'd read, but they deserve to have themselves mentioned in writing somewhere, even if it's just in here. I miss you all, and thank you for taking care of our town.

Thank you, everyone. I'll see you in the next book.

James Kuckkan writes stories and essays. He lives in a library on the second floor of one of Iowa City's most distinguished former communes. In his free time, he enjoys hiking, baking peanut butter cookies, and reading and writing manifestos. You can find him at "James Kuckkan writes here."

Jayne Costello is an artist, illustrator, and graphic designer based out of Hartland, Wisconsin. In her free time, she enjoys drawing, going on walks with her dog Sully, and listening to the *Mad Max: Fury Road* soundtrack in order to feel something. You can find her at https://costelloj1997.wixsite.com/website.

The End.